Praise for *The End of Longing*

The End of Longing is a cleverly written piece of historical fiction…a complex story of mystery and intrigue… I was completely absorbed from the first page until the final scene. *Bookseller and Publisher*

Reid scores a considerable success in recreating the hardscrabble frontier towns of an age that is increasingly alien to our own. The reader encounters a pageant of nineteenth-century lives here…a realistic portrait of a bleak world. *Australian Book Review*

The End of Longing is distinguished by its sense of place, which is ironic really, as one of the themes in this richly layered book is that of travel and the peripatetic lives of the married couple at the centre of the story. But wherever his characters go, be it Japan, Canada or Honolulu, Ian Reid places us vividly there. *The Age*

Reid's fine and unusual historical novel concerns a man who is a fugitive not only from the law and his past misdeeds but perhaps more essentially from his repressed better nature. Maybe – as Reid subtly suggests – it is the desire for revenge against the angels of his own nature that Hammond self-destructively seeks. *The Australian*

A tale rich in historical detail, creating two memorable and affecting main characters. *The West Australian*

Skilfully realised… How well does any person know the 'truth' of another? This question underpins much of the novel and keeps the reader turning the pages… The gradual revelation of clues allows the reader to become the detective in pursuit of truth. *Transnational Literature*

Compelling… intense… poetic… it stayed with me and has been hard to shake off. *Sydney Morning Herald*

Loved it! Great mix of history, travel, and psychological study. Clever and engrossing. *Goodreads*

Praise for *That Untravelled World*

Perth comes alive in Reid's hands, and throughout the book Western Australia's regional towns are deftly depicted… We are persuaded to ask to what extent we can let unfair disadvantage dictate how we live the remainder of our lives. *The Australian*

It is beautifully written and eminently readable… I enjoyed the finely balanced structure of the story, its accuracy, restrained telling, and the way in which the era, age and physicality of the character, at various stages of his life, was so clearly evoked. *Iris Lavell Blogspot*

Set predominantly in Perth's southern riverside suburbs in the early 1900s, *That Untravelled World* paints a vivid picture of the area at the time. Harry's tale of early confidence followed by recurrent disappointment is evocative of the period in which it is set. With its rapid technological change and economic ups and downs, it's a period that resonates with our own. *The West Australian*

This has everything – snippets of Perth's history, lots of philosophy, a little geography and marvellous descriptions… Ian Reid acquaints us with our own journey into the 'untravelled' world of our aspirations, and the life experiences encountered as we struggle with broken dreams and upheavals on our way to becoming older and wiser. Buy this book – you won't be disappointed. *Have A Go*

Reid has deftly woven some fascinating WA history into the narrative, giving a very vivid and familiar sense of Perth in days gone by. This history provides a fitting backdrop to a story that is compelling and satisfyingly unpredictable. *Writing WA*

This fine novel presents a story faithful to its period. It covers the gamut of human emotion, from passion to apathy, ecstasy to dysphoria, sacrifice to indulgence, and love to racism. *Bonzer*

That Untravelled World draws the reader into a walk through time… Dreams and disillusion, difficult and concealed family relationships, regional disenfranchisement, the tyranny of distance, as well as the pros and cons of technological advancement… They are themes that speak to our present society. *Trust News Australia*

Praise for *The Mind's Own Place*

The author's prose is always vivid and evocative, almost poetic. The dialogue, moral dilemmas and contradictions are all handled with equally exquisite expression. It's been a long time since I came to the end of a novel and immediately wanted to read it again to uncover more of its nuances. Ian Reid is a revelation, and deserves the widest recognition as a remarkable ambassador for Australian historical fiction. *Historical Novels Review (U.K.)*

A great gathering of personality, character after character, in irreducible and fully imagined life… In *The Mind's Own Place* Ian Reid gives us the 'life-surplus' of history: love and journeys and work and ideas, fear and purposeful action and sometimes failure, all playing out before us in this big and beautifully balanced novel of character. *Rochford Street Review*

Reid richly evokes the abandoned English worlds of those who travel to the antipodes, whose loss is therefore the more poignant. Turn by turn he engages us with his characters' untidy and unruly fates in an assured work of historical reconstruction and imagination. *The Australian*

A compelling portrait of Perth's beginnings… mastery of story-telling… ability to capture the machinations of the mind. *Have A Go*

Reid's vivid writing and attention to historical detail result in settings and characters that make for an enthralling and immersive reading experience. *Writing WA*

A captivating tale… incorporates a strong sense of place.
The Post

Compelling fictional characters leap off the page with all the veracity of their historical counterparts… It is historical detective fiction and social commentary rolled into one. The texture shimmers. *The West Australian*

Praise for *A Thousand Tongues*

A Thousand Tongues is a novel of ideas … impeccably researched, meticulously plotted, and blessed with elegantly and artfully crafted prose. Nothing is laboured, and the pages slip by in a most beguiling manner. *Rochford Street Review*

Great story told with great humanity. This is a thoughtful, readable, and sensitively written book of interconnected tales. Each time period is vividly described with great attention to the values and racial distinctions of that era. We share the characters' deepest experiences and feel viscerally the reactions of others. We are different afterwards. *Amazon* (five stars)

Ian Reid twists together three tales in an examination of conscience demonstrating that "what is right" is rarely a singular narrative or universal truth… The fate of those who question their conscience and judge themselves unworthy weaves the three narratives together in the uncomfortable inconvenient truth that is human experience. *A Thousand Tongues* is a story that twists and turns to provoke thought and discussion.
Writing WA

This Australian writer knows how to tell a story well, and has done his research well. It is a first-class read exploring themes of conscience and racial tension and the legacies of guilt and shame. *Dartmoor News*

With its main focus on how conscience played out in the past and how it impacts the present, the story will certainly open one's eyes ... A fine and complex novel that will give the reader much thought. *Historical Novels Review (U.K.)*

ABOUT THE AUTHOR

IAN REID is the author of fifteen books – novels, poetry and several kinds of non-fiction. His writings have been translated into five languages and won international acclaim including the Antipodes Prize for poetry. *The Madwoman's Coat* is his fifth historical novel. Born in New Zealand, he now lives in Perth and is an Adjunct Professor in English and Literary Studies at the University of Western Australia. His website 'Reid on Writing' is at www.ianreid-author.com

The Madwoman's Coat

Ian Reid

FRAME WORK PRESS

First published in 2021 by
Framework Press
27 Cunningham Street, Ardross,
Western Australia 6153
www.frameworkpress.com.au

A catalogue record for this
book is available from the
National Library of Australia

978-0-6485223-2-4 (pbk)
978-0-6485223-3-1 (ebk)

Cover images: Riddarateppid, National Museum of Iceland;
Woman Sewing by Susan Macdowell Eakins,
Pennsylvania Academy of the Fine Arts.
(For detailed acknowledgements, see final page of Afterword.)
Cover and book design: Steve Barwick

For Gale

I made my song a coat
Covered with embroideries
Out of old mythologies
From heel to throat;
But the fools caught it,
Wore it in the world's eyes
As though they'd wrought it.
Song, let them take it,
For there's more enterprise
In walking naked.

W.B. Yeats, *A Coat*

Fremantle
1897

ONE

---

*H*ANDS CLASPED BEHIND HIS BACK AS IF TO KEEP THEM
uncontaminated, Charles Whittle leaned forward
gingerly towards the body, which sat half-upright on
the bed with a scissor blade buried deep in the slender neck.
Dim morning light entering the narrow cell through a small
barred window was enough for the Superintendent to see that
gouts of blood had spurted not only over Isabella Trent's plain
nightgown and coarse blanket but also on parts of the extraordinary piece of clothing spread across her lap and knees: an
ornately embroidered frock coat. Stooping, grimacing, Whittle
peered in perplexity at the decorative details.

'An astonishing piece! What do you make of it, Matron?'

'Very curious indeed. Why cover a man's large black coat with
feminine embellishments? I can see she was stitching away on
it at the time of being attacked, poor soul. Fingers clenched on
the needle, and there's her little sewing box, look, knocked down
on the floor.'

She was about to add that this garment would doubtless be
the same one she herself had permitted a certain visitor to bring

in here years ago, before anything was sewn onto it – but Whittle pushed ahead with his own line of thought.

'How on earth could she produce such a thing without your knowledge? Or anyone's knowledge, presumably?'

Mrs Higgs straightened her bonnet and cleared her throat before replying. Though the Medical Superintendent was not an unkind man, his dour manner often made her defensive.

'Must have done it by candlelight, Doctor, night after night. Mind, she was always secretive during the daytime hours, too, despite being required, of course, to go out into the grassy enclosure every afternoon, like all the others, except for a few months when she did some sewing for Mrs Samson. Wouldn't ever join any games or gardening. Sequestered herself as much as possible. Exceptionally clever with a needle, I knew that, but to do all this intricate work and somehow keep it hidden for what was probably a very long while – well, she could only have managed it when others were asleep. Not so difficult, on account of being confined after supper to her separate cell, a good way along the corridor from the dormitory where most of the patients have their beds.'

Whittle frowned, gesturing at the coat. 'What's the point of this thing, anyhow? Plenty of skill in it, I suppose, but some of the decoration looks…quite outlandish, don't you think? I can't imagine who'd want to wear such queer garb. Whatever possessed her to devise it? An outpouring of sheer madness, is it?' He wrinkled his nose.

'Unless it's a kind of puzzle, deliberately contrived? Perhaps a message to decipher, could it be? Or something entirely private, done just to occupy her mind, like talking to herself?'

'We may never know, I suppose.' Whittle stared at it, shaking his head unhappily. As he glanced back at the inconvenient corpse, his lip twitched with annoyance and the grooves deepened in his forehead. People would think a nasty incident like this reflected badly on his supervision of the Fremantle Asylum.

A brisker tone: 'Everything exactly as you found it, Matron?'

'Oh exactly. Nothing's been touched, I assure you.'

'So the cell door was open like this, with its key left in the lock?'

'Just as they are, Doctor.'

'And no sign, you say, of the orderly who was on duty – what's her name?'

'Mack. Elsie Mack. Vanished without a trace.'

'I'll notify Mr Fairbairn immediately. He won't be able to hold an inquest before Monday but I dare say the verdict is going to be plain enough, as Mack was the one who had a key to the cell. Apparently, for whatever reason, she must have killed this woman some time between your two regular nocturnal rounds, and then bolted. Your entry in the Occurrence Book says Mack was at her post at half past eleven last night but not at 4 a.m. So deciding what happened should be a straightforward matter, then – though no doubt the Coroner will want to hear your thoughts, Mrs Higgs, on the whys and wherefores.'

'I'm at a loss to think of any motive. Completely at a loss. There'd been no friction between the two, as far as I'm aware. Elsie Mack has always seemed a reliable assistant. Perhaps slow-witted, that's the worst I'd say of her. Never a hint of violence. As for Miss Trent, well, she was certainly an unusual person, very intense in her emotions, but not hostile. You're aware of the circumstances of her committal.'

'Yes, yes. Not hostile, you say. Yet she did sometimes provoke conflict, didn't she?'

'Not generally, no, though you may be remembering that there was one peculiar incident several years ago. Of course, many of our inmates will fly into a rage over nothing. Become wildly demented, some of them. Kicking, scratching, biting, quite ferocious. Even a few of the chronic imbeciles, harmless enough most of the time, can get extremely upset now and then, lashing out at one another. But Miss Trent kept to herself as much as she could, and apart from that one episode a long while back she gave the orderlies no trouble, as far as I know. Shocking she should die so violently.'

'So we have a pair of mysteries, then. Why did Mack do such a terrible thing to her, and what purpose did Trent have in producing this strangely embroidered coat?'

'Underneath those questions,' the Matron added diffidently, 'there's also something mysterious about Isabella Trent herself. Not only her background. The character of the poor woman, too: so hard to fathom.'

Pensive, Whittle stroked his whiskers in a slow caress. 'Is there anyone who might shed light on such matters? Anyone who should be summoned to the inquest, apart from ourselves and a police officer?'

'The sole person who ever came to see Miss Trent, all this time she's been in here, is Tilly Carter. That's Mrs Matilda Carter; calls herself Tilly.'

'I've seen her here, I think,' said Whittle. 'Dumpy? Rubicund cheeks?'

'That's the one. She may know something, if anyone does, being such a regular visitor. Once a fortnight, year in year out, all the way from Guildford, twenty miles to Fremantle on the railway and then back again. Quite a journey for a lady who's getting elderly now.'

'Some family connection with the dead woman?'

'Not as far as I know. Just a loyal friend, I believe. It was from Mrs Carter, by the way, that poor Miss Trent got this coat, not long after she came into the Asylum. Back before you took over from Dr Brampton. She's the only inmate allowed to have extra clothing here. Special permission given because of the unusual circumstances when she was committed. But I hadn't seen the coat for many a day, and forgot about it. Probably concealed under her mattress during the day.'

'We need to get a telegraph message to Mrs Carter straight away about attending Monday's inquest. I'll visit Mr Fairbairn now to arrange that. A police deposition will be required, of course, and I'd have thought an officer would be here by now to see the cell, make notes for a report and so forth, before you call in the undertaker for funeral arrangements. When did you send a message to the station?'

'Nearly two hours ago.'

'Where's the fellow got to? It'll be that new young constable, I suppose – what's his name – Ashby?'

'Ashton. Perhaps the message hasn't reached him yet. He could be away from the station, with so much happening around here this week. Do you think Inspector Rowe may be available? I heard he's in town because of all the Jubilee events – quietly keeping an eye on safety for the Governor and other officials, making sure nothing gets out of hand with the processions and such. Most of that's over now, so he could be asked to help us here. The fact that he knew Miss Trent...'

'Ah – did he? How so?'

'Well, you see, he interviewed her when she was taken into custody, years ago.'

'Indeed? All right, I should be able to get an urgent message to him through Mr Fairbairn. Can't twiddle our thumbs waiting for Ashton to turn up. If Rowe is nearby, and able to come promptly, I'd much prefer to have him on the case. Clever man, dependable. And he'd waste no time in getting a search under way for your Elsie Mack. Meanwhile you're to stay with the body, Matron. Keep others away from it. And from the madwoman's coat.'

Superintendent Whittle left in his usual abrupt way. Settling herself, Mrs Higgs kept her eyes averted from the victim's fearfully twisted expression and gory neck but looked closely at the coat. You couldn't call something so delicately done a hodge-podge, she thought, but the mixture of styles and hues and materials disconcerted her. Attached along the sleeves were oblong pieces of linen, whose bright borders carried a chain of small linked oval medallions, each enclosing a tiny appliqué floral motif. The wide collar was quite different in manner: it had a ground fabric of dark blue velvet, meticulously embroidered with gilt thread in the form of slender coiling tendrils and large star-like flowers.

Although the virtuosity of those ornamentations on collar and sleeves seemed finer and more ingenious than in any piece of needlework the Matron had ever seen before, it was the back of the coat that compelled her attention. Covering the whole area from the shoulders down to the knee-length base was a large full-breadth panel, cross-stitched with multi-coloured woollen yarns and elegant touches of silk in a pattern of red, blue-black and white against a yellow background. Its elaborate design, still eye-catching despite the bloodstains, featured human and animal shapes set individually in octagonal frames. Most of them were mounted horsemen, cavaliers in formal attire, but at the midpoint of the design, larger than the surrounding men, was a startling image of a woman. This central figure seemed so wanton that the Matron, though not easily shocked, turned her gaze quickly to other aspects of the panel.

It was not only the profusion of pictures, patterns and emblems that made it all such a conundrum. There was also the lettering. Mrs Higgs couldn't make much sense of it. Around the inner edge of the collar, stitched in compact capitals but barely discernible in the cell's murky light, were two personal names followed by a little word that seemed at first to express piety, oddly placed: ISABELLA LUCY GOD. The Matron took a closer look. No, not God – it was Gud. Gud? What could that mean – a quaint surname, was it? And was Lucy a separate person?

Avoiding the crimson smears, Mrs Higgs ran her finger-tips over the surface of the panel, feeling its different textures. Where had all these pieces of fabric come from, and these many colourful threads? Although sewing was a common activity for several of the other inmates, their work had nothing fancy about it. The simplest materials sufficed for ordinary oven cloths and gloves, cushion covers, handkerchiefs, other minor practical articles for domestic use, or for a few humble samplers coarsely stitched. This spectacular coat evoked a different world, inscrutable, far removed from those humdrum items.

To Mrs Higgs, distressed that this terrible thing had disrupted her domain, it was a comfort to see Detective Inspector Rowe arriving to examine the scene of the crime. Old Runty Rowe must be getting towards retirement, she thought, but his familiar homespun appearance – short stocky build, the same

rolling gait, that thick moustache now streaked with white –
had something reassuring in it, and she knew she could trust
the decency of his character. Though a resolute enforcer of the
law, with a gruff turn of phrase, he had earned popular esteem
as a fair-minded penny-plain sort of man. She herself knew how
considerately he had dealt with some of the luckless wretches
whose transgressions brought them by way of the judicial
system into this refuge, and she remembered in particular his
unobtrusive compassion towards Isabella Trent at the time of
her sensational arrest and committal years ago. He was about
to find out that the very same woman was the one whose death
he had now come to investigate, and the Matron felt sure his
discovery of the victim's identity would trouble him more than
he was likely to admit. Her message early this morning to the
police station had been brief: merely that a female inmate had
died violently and the attendant on duty in this wing had disappeared. No names.

'Well, Matron,' said Rowe as she conducted him towards
the cell where the body waited, 'I can let you know this: your
missing orderly isn't the only one who's got away.'

From the men's wing of the Asylum, he told her, Thomas
Ramsay had absconded during the night. She knew that Ramsay,
like the other three male attendants and unlike the pair of free
women employed in her own wing, was a convict awaiting his
ticket-of-leave discharge and deemed sufficiently trustworthy
to be assigned in the meantime to the Asylum as an assistant
warder. Now, by bolting, he had ruined his chance of an early
release. Once recaptured, as he surely would be, he could expect
a doubling of his sentence.

Rowe sighed at the folly of it. 'So recklessly impatient, some
of these convicts,' he said. 'They don't have the brains to think

ahead. Where does this Ramsay imagine he can go? If he lingers around settled areas or tries to get away on a ship, he'll soon be caught, and if he heads off into the inland bush he'll starve. There's nowhere to go out there. A big lot of nowhere. He's persuaded one of your orderlies to go with him, by the look of it. More fool her!'

'I suppose she thought,' said the Matron, 'being so plainly guilty of this murder, she had no choice but to flee. Could be it was Mack persuaded Ramsay to help her escape justice.'

'You're sure she's the killer?'

'Who else? Mack had the key to the cell.'

'But why would she do it?'

'As to that, I've no idea, Inspector.' She stopped, raising her hand. They had reached the cell. 'Something to tell you before you go in. The dead woman – you'll recognise her. Every inmate is a sorry case, God knows, but this one especially. I've often wondered whether she was really insane at all. Such intelligent eyes, yet most of the time she'd retreat into herself, seldom saying a word, never letting us glimpse more than fragments of her full story.'

'It's not…?' Rowe left his half-formed question hanging as he turned quickly to enter the cell.

TWO

G UARDED BY CONSTABLE ASHTON, ELSIE MACK SAT
fidgeting and snivelling at the back of the dismal little
room, eyes downcast, miserably waiting her turn to be
interrogated.

'Quick work apprehending her, Inspector,' whispered Whittle
to Rowe. 'No sign of Ramsay yet?'

Rowe shook his grizzled head. 'But he won't be far away.
Mack says he abandoned her when she baulked at leaving the
Rockingham road to strike out into the bush with him. A search
party's on his heels.'

Whittle began to ask whether Mack had confessed to the
crime, but there was no time for further conversation: a hush
fell on the room as Robert Fairbairn entered, his stern face
framed authoritatively by an eyebrow hedge and a broad spade
of beard. He needed no show of pomp to augment his grave
demeanour. The three jurors, nondescript, followed meekly and
sat on a bench to his left. Having presided over many an inquest
during his tenure as Fremantle's resident magistrate, Fairbairn
was well regarded for his calmly deliberative manner. A just and

wise man – everyone said so. A diligent servant of the colony. The small group present on this occasion knew that it would be nearly his last duty before leaving for an upcountry posting.

Matron Martha Higgs, the first witness to be called, deposed that she had known the deceased, Isabella Trent, since the latter's committal seven years earlier. In the early stages of her detention, said the Matron, Miss Trent had been prone to sudden outbursts of turbulent feelings; but increasingly she chose to withdraw into a stubborn silence. Asked by the Coroner why, if this woman had become quiet for the most part, it was still considered necessary to keep her in a solitary cell rather than in the open dormitory, Mrs Higgs disclosed that some of the wilder inmates, interpreting Trent's tight-lipped habit as contemptuous of them, felt provoked by it into angry antagonism. Some were also fiercely resentful at what they saw as favourable treatment of Miss Trent. So she was confined, for her own protection, to a separate cell.

Was there any factual basis, Mr Fairbairn wanted to know, for thinking this person to have been favoured in some way? After hesitating, the Matron made a candid admission: she herself had felt deeply sympathetic to Isabella Trent's plight, and inclined to alleviate it in small ways, believing that she didn't deserve her long incarceration. Indeed the Matron's personal view, she declared, was that the judicial system had dealt harshly with this unfortunate woman at the time of her trial, probably because of her accuser's position in the community.

Flexing his thick eyebrows in reproof, the Coroner interrupted to remark that while he knew Mrs Higgs's opinion on this matter was shared by some others, he could not condone public criticism of a previous court decision, particularly one that had no direct bearing on the present inquest. He instructed the two journalists in the room that their newspaper reports must make no mention of this contentious part of the Matron's statement.

Mrs Higgs concluded by describing briefly how she found Miss Trent's lifeless body in the unlocked cell at about 4 a.m. last Saturday morning, soon after discovering that that the orderly on duty, Elsie Mack, had gone missing.

Next to testify was Dr Charles Whittle, Medical Superintendent, who said he could add little to the Matron's account. It was his usual practice, he explained, to visit the Asylum each morning, first the female wing, then the male wing. Informed by Mrs Higgs upon his arrival last Saturday that a patient had died violently during the night, he entered the cell, inspected the corpse and noted its gashed throat. He then checked the Occurrence Book. He believed that the disappearance of Elsie Mack, who had been entrusted with the keys, plainly indicated her guilt, though it was not clear why she murdered the hapless Miss Trent.

At this, there was a snuffling whimper from Elsie Mack, and the Coroner raised a reproachful hand as he reminded Whittle that the judicial process had yet to determine questions of culpability in this case.

He then called on Mrs Matilda Carter, plump as a suet pudding, who gave evidence that she had become a friend of Isabella Trent soon after the younger woman's arrival in the colony, when Dr Raymond Oram, Mrs Carter's Guildford neighbour, employed Miss Trent as a housekeeper.

'So she was a servant in the house next door. A station quite different to yours. Then how did the friendship develop?' the Coroner enquired.

'Well, you see, being a widow myself, and Miss Trent being a spinster new to the town, each of us was glad of the other's company whenever she had a little free time. Although she was in domestic service, she spoke well and must have had a good education, I think. An unusual sort of person. Occasionally we'd have a pot of tea together, and a scone or two.'

'She had no family here in Western Australia, to your knowledge?'

'None, sir – nor back in England, not mentioned anyhow. An orphan, she told me, and no brothers or sisters.'

'Are you aware of anything else about Miss Trent's background that may have a bearing on her situation here?'

'She didn't ever talk directly about the circumstances that brought her to the colony, and I didn't like to press her. I did wonder whether there might have been a courtship that went awry, something of that sort... Such an attractive young woman, you see, but no word of any beau, and seemed to be angry towards men generally. I once happened to say a nephew of mine was a handsome lad, and she made such a scoffing comment I decided to steer clear of that topic from then on. Certainly guarded her privacy, she did. All I know, really, about her life before she emigrated is what she told me when I praised a quite exceptional piece of needlework she showed me. Isabella Trent was no mere seamstress, you see, but what I'd call a real artist, proud of her skill, and she'd learnt fine embroidery as a girl in her home town – I forget where she said that was – and later honed her craft in London.'

'Can you tell us anything, Mrs Carter, about the embroidered coat on the table in front of you?'

'Oh yes indeed. I was the one who brought the coat into the Asylum for her. That was because the poor creature felt desperately chilled when she was put here. I remember how she kept rubbing her thin hands, said her bones were aching with the cold – I can hear her now, in her misery, repeating that word – cold, cold – and the odd way it sounded in her mouth, rhyming with snowed. Her accent, you see. Well, she'd lost so much flesh after her arrest, what with the shock of it and the worry I suppose, and refusing to eat properly. When I saw her, first visit, she was shivering, poor skinny wretch. It was a bitter winter, and the nights would have been cruel in such a stony draughty place. I spoke right away to the Matron, who kindly agreed that Miss Trent deserved special consideration. To be quite frank, we both thought the court had treated her badly – I'm sorry, sir, I can see you don't like my saying it, but I must. She was a good person, quite unusual in some ways but not a lunatic, that's my honest opinion.'

Frowning censoriously, Fairbairn cleared his throat and tapped the desk with an admonitory forefinger. 'The coat, Mrs Carter. You were telling us about the coat.'

'Yes. Well. So I brought in a frock coat for her, one that my late husband used to wear. Good thick woollen fabric, double-breasted. It would have kept her warm through those chilly nights in her cell.'

'But the decoration?'

'Oh, I had no idea she was embroidering the coat. No idea. But glancing at it now, I can certainly tell you where all the threads and panels of cloth came from. On many of my visits, over the years, I'd bring along various sewing materials for her so that she could while away the empty time with her fine needle-work. Never crossed my mind she'd use them to embellish this garment. Not that it would have troubled me one whit. What she's done here is quite beautiful, if you ask me. Strange, admittedly, and it would have startled my husband to see it, I can tell you! But beautiful.'

As Mrs Carter brought her testimony to an end, an emerald parrot flashed into the room through an open door, squeaking in panic as it flew this way and that until it sped straight against a window, plummeted to the floor and lay there motionless, the black head askew, the gold-ringed neck broken. The loud thump of its head striking the glass made people flinch but within a few moments the bird was forgotten; all eyes switched to Inspector Rowe, now stepping forward to make his statement.

Though posted to Geraldton years earlier, Runty Rowe remained well known around Fremantle. After almost three decades in Western Australia, much of it based in this port town, everyone had an opinion about him – mostly approbatory. The colony's first detective, and still generally viewed as the best. There'd been a couple of controversial episodes; he'd come in for criticism from some quarters for getting friendly with dubious figures like Satan Browne, but that was a while back, and besides, in the popular view it did him credit that he disregarded rumour and reputation in his dealings with people of every stripe. The word was, he looked at you without prejudice, whoever you were. Inclined to give you the benefit of the doubt. Considered the facts fairly and made up his own mind.

With an air of effortless composure, Rowe now began his evidence by explaining that he had become involved in this case as a matter of chance. Happening to be back in Fremantle for a few days after a long absence, he had gone to the Asylum on Saturday at the request of Dr Whittle to look into the unlawful death of an inmate and the disappearance of an orderly.

'This inmate, it transpired, was previously known to you?'

'Yes. My first encounter with Isabella Trent was some seven years ago, when – as on the present occasion – I'd come back south for a short period of leave from my position in Geraldton.'

'The circumstances of your first encounter with her, Inspector?'

'The Guildford police station requested my help with a difficult situation. A young woman taken into custody was in an extremely disturbed state. Miss Trent. Furious, they said. There had been a scandalous incident in the street, leading to her detention. She was making serious allegations, which the local officer was inclined to regard as hysterical but thought it prudent to investigate with my assistance. At first she was deeply mistrustful. After some time I was able to calm her down. Winning her confidence became easier when she recognised something in my way of speaking that showed I'd come from Staffordshire, as she did. I got her talking about her home town, a few miles upbank from where I used to live in the Potteries. Anyhow, I managed after that to persuade her to tell her side of the story. But of course Dr Oram put forward a very different version of events. Accusation and counter-accusation.'

Rowe paused theatrically before asking the Coroner whether, for the present purpose, it was necessary to summarise Isabella Trent's subsequent trial and its outcome, probably well known already to those present.

'Not necessary,' said Fairbairn. 'Please describe now, in brief, the scene that confronted you on Saturday when you entered the cell occupied by the deceased.'

'It was obvious to me at once that Miss Trent had been murdered during the night. The fatal wound could not possibly have been self-inflicted, either on purpose or by accident. Her cell door was unlocked, I presume by the assailant. I ascertained that the person on duty that night and therefore entrusted with the keys was Elsie Mack, who had evidently absconded, as had one of the male orderlies, Thomas Ramsay. Thinking it most likely that they had gone southwards together, I arranged for a search party from Rockingham to watch the road in that direction. An officer apprehended Mack yesterday morning. We know that Ramsay can't be far from the point where she was found, and I'm confident he'll be seized before long.'

The last person to be cross-examined was Elsie Mack. A welter of words and sobs soon tumbled from her trembling lips. She was horrified, she said, quite horrified, to learn that Miss Trent had been killed. She insisted that she herself had no knowledge of this dreadful event until Inspector Rowe told her about it. She had no reason to wish poor Miss Trent any harm, truly, none at all, and would never, never have hurt her. On the night when she ran off with Mr Ramsay – wanting to live with him and not having the forbearance to wait for his ticket of leave, never guessing that he would abandon her before a day had passed – she hadn't gone anywhere near Miss Trent's cell. She had placed the set of keys on the duty desk before leaving. Someone else must have taken them and entered Miss Trent's cell…

Following a strong hint from the Coroner, the jury soon decided that despite her dereliction of duty – a serious offence which had contributed indirectly to the death of an inmate and would disqualify her from further employment – Elsie Mack was nonetheless a credible witness in the matter of primary concern to this inquest. It seemed entirely improbable that she had killed Isabella Trent, having had no discernible motive for doing so. The verdict: 'murder by a person or persons unknown.'

THREE

———

*T*ILLY CARTER'S MELANCHOLY MOOD PERSISTED ALL THE way back home from the funeral. Such occasions were never cheerful but this one left her more profoundly saddened than she'd felt for many a year. A decade ago, when her husband Fred died after an implacable illness, there was at least the consoling thought that he'd reached his threescore-and-ten with a full measure of contentment. Wilting physically but sturdy in spirit, Fred came to the end of his days aware of being loved and respected, and her own knowledge of this had been a comfort as she glanced around the ample crowd attending his obsequies. No such solace for the handful of mourners at Isabella Trent's token ceremony.

The whole business was over in no time at all. They had gathered first in the Asylum's garden as a faint drizzle floated on the westerly breeze. The chaplain murmured some perfunctory prayers and read the 23rd Psalm (But surely goodness and mercy *didn't* follow *you*, my poor dear, thought Tilly). After that, a small procession accompanied the narrow coffin to the church burial ground nearby: Superintendent Whittle walking beside the chaplain, Matron Higgs and an orderly next behind them, then Tilly herself with Inspector Rowe, and just half a dozen of the inmates shuffling morosely at the rear. More prayers, more blather about merciful providence, and finally the doleful formula 'committing the mortal remains of our sister Isabella Trent to the ground, earth to earth, ashes to ashes, dust to dust, in sure and certain hope of the resurrection…' Hope? Had Isabella ever known its blessings? Her ashes now committed to the ground, just as her living body had been so wrongly committed to the Asylum years before.

After the funeral, leaning on her cane, Tilly had a subdued, desultory conversation with the Inspector and the Matron, conscious that they knew even less than she did about the dead woman, and was then about to leave for the railway station when Charles Whittle handed her the coat, turned inside out, rolled into a bulky bundle and tied with string.

'This belongs to you now, I suppose,' he said with a shrug. 'If to anyone.'

During the tiresome rail journey from Fremantle to Perth and on to Guildford, she held the large package firmly on her lap. The journey was one that she had made so frequently for so long that she now felt an odd mixture of relief and regret at the thought that she would never be making it again. That evening, beside the kitchen fireplace in her bentwood rocking chair, resting her swollen ankles on a footstool, she unpicked the knotted string and unfolded the remnant of Isabella's life. When exhibited at the inquest it had been a splendid curiosity, something to admire from a formal distance; now she could examine its texture closely, turning the garment round and round in a slow process of reverential scrutiny. What a marvellous, mysterious thing it was, this coat of many colours! Such refined patterning, so much delicate needlework – and yet seemingly interlaced with riddles.

Thinking of all the pieces of fabric and reels of thread she had so often taken with her on those countless visits to the Asylum, Tilly recalled something her sister Jane had said in one of her letters – well meant but inapposite. It was more than 30 years since the siblings last saw each other, Melbourne being so far away from Perth, but they often exchanged letters, and Jane, a Quaker, made a habit of passing on various snippets from her earnest reading, which included passages from Elizabeth Fry's popular memoirs about the enterprise of prison reform. When Tilly described to Jane her own practice of visiting the Fremantle Lunatic Asylum and supplying Isabella with materials for embroidery work, Jane copied out for her sister some of Mrs Fry's edifying remarks on needlework as a suitably reformative occupation for incarcerated women, and on the provision of sewing equipment to female prisoners travelling on convict ships to Australia.

This, Tilly knew, was hardly applicable to Isabella's situation, though trying to explain the point to Jane would be a waste of time. The simple kind of morally improving handicraft envisaged by Elizabeth Fry, while it may have been a useful way to keep malefactors occupied during a long jail sentence or shipboard voyage, had little to do with Isabella's baffling artistry.

Shifting her weight from haunch to haunch, rubbing at the ache in her hip as the chair moved gently to and fro, Tilly stared at each segment and minutely executed detail of the large panel on the back of the frock coat. All the meticulous work that must have gone into these designs, all the painstaking eye-straining precision of it, done by the meagre light of a small flickering flame, hour after hour, night after night! And then Isabella would have carefully stowed the coat away before each cell inspection.

Tilly's gaze kept returning to the panel's dominant figure: a brazenly naked woman sat astride a horse – no, it was a deer, its antlers entangled in the branches of a flowering tree. What could this represent? Some obscure old story from literature or folklore or myth? And why had Isabella included such a queer scene, bemusing and somehow disquieting, at the very centre of the design?

She turned her attention to the collar, with its mystifying trio of names around the inner rim. ISABELLA LUCY GUD. It occurred to her that the last of these might be incomplete, because immediately following the D there was a loose bit of broken thread, perhaps the start of another letter. It could even be this name, interrupted, that Isabella had been working on at the moment of her sudden death.

Lucy... It stirred some vague association in a corner of Tilly's mind, and after a few minutes she managed to remember where she had seen the name. It was written inside a book belonging to Isabella, one of her very few possessions, entrusted to Tilly's care years before. Getting up stiffly from her chair, she shuffled into the parlour and searched along the shelves of the bookcase. There it was, *The Lovers of Gudrun*. Gudrun! Surely this must be the name intended by the fragmentary portion of lettering stitched on the coat collar. Tilly opened the book and read an inscription on the flyleaf: 'To my dear friend Lucy, with affectionate thoughts from May.' In this increasingly complicated puzzle, who were May and Lucy, how was Isabella linked with them, and why was Gudrun's incomplete name linked with those of Lucy and Isabella herself on the collar?

The Lovers of Gudrun, its title page proclaimed, was by William Morris, excerpted from *The Earthly Paradise* and reprinted in 1870 as a separate poem. Turning the first few pages, Tilly found its old-fashioned phrasing difficult but could see from a scatter of names that the story it recounted was set in some foreign land, probably in the far north: there were places called Herdholt, Bathstead and Laxriver, and characters with names like Olaf, Thorgerd and Skallagrim.

That Isabella cherished the book had been obvious. So when asked to take care of it for her, Tilly responded with a question: 'But won't you want to have it with you while you're locked away?'

'No no,' said Isabella. 'Too precious. I want it kept safe. In the Asylum it could easily be damaged by patients or confiscated by orderlies. I'll still be able to hold its poetry secure inside me, because I memorised long passages while I was travelling out to Australia.'

Tilly didn't doubt that Isabella could recite many lines of verse to herself from memory. Early in their acquaintance the younger woman had revealed a prodigious ability to store words and images in her heart, retrieving them at will. When they compared what they could recall of their respective voyages to Australia, Tilly had lamented the fact that her own impressions were relatively meagre. 'I was just a young thing at the time, suffering from sickness most of the way, so I've no clear recollection except of being cooped up in a small malodorous cabin.' But for Isabella every aspect of her journey remained vivid. Picturing it all in her mind's eye with precision and full colour, as if people and scenes were being projected from magic lantern slides, she told Tilly about several companions among the four dozen young women emigrating with her under the auspices of the same organisation; about their massive ship, the S.S. *Nairnshire*, a newly built iron screw steamer; about the London dockyard strike, looming when the passengers went on board, which would have prevented their departure if it had come an hour or two earlier; about the increasingly squalid conditions in steerage, and the singing and card games that helped to distract them from their discomfort; about the clamorous complaints from cattle and boarhounds at all hours; about the two deaths at sea, first the cook's collapse with heat stroke ('Our food improved after that') and then the shocking action of a thin young man who calmly handed his fob watch and wallet to a seaman before leaping from the deck to sink into the spume; about the heavy squalls that sent high cross seas sweeping over the ship fore and aft; about the frolics of countless flying fish when the weather grew calmer; and much more. Threaded through all these reminiscences and through other conversations, there would be striking phrases that Isabella seemed to draw from a plentiful store of poetry shelved in her head. Musingly, with an abstracted air, she spoke in murmurs of 'ruinous victory,' of 'slow-foot time,' of 'interwoven miseries.'

In those occasional talks around the teapot when the two women were getting acquainted, Isabella's manner was usually lively, even verging on the voluble, though from time to time she would slip silently into private reflection. Tilly remembered the sparkle in her new friend's eyes, the exuberance in her voice, the animation in her gestures; and less often, briefly glimpsed, there were flittering shadows. Tilly would chatter freely about the ups and downs of her own life – a strict upbringing in Chelmsford, marriage to Fred, the decision to emigrate, her sorrow at being unable to bear children, Fred's gradual success as a merchant and then his long bodily decline and eventual death – but Isabella never reciprocated with anecdotes about her personal background. Constraint was no less palpable for being unacknowledged.

About her employer and his household, Isabella said little – not that Tilly had tried to solicit any gossip. All of Guildford's townsfolk felt that they knew Dr Oram. He was cautiously respected in the local community, enjoying the combined prestige of medical practitioner, parish church stalwart, self-assured paterfamilias (quite eclipsing his wife), and owner of one of the town's most elegant properties. A man of substance and gentility, who carried himself accordingly. Inclined to be distant in manner, yes, even haughty, but surely his social position warranted that.

Although Isabella had counted herself lucky to be hired by the Oram family almost immediately after arriving in the colony, there was no false modesty about her. In her interview it must have been easy to make a favourable impression. She wrote and spoke more fluently, more self-confidently, than most of the young women seeking work could have managed. A quick intelligence shone effortlessly through her words.

It was in Padbury's General Store that Tilly had first encountered her neighbour's new servant. Overhearing this young woman as she ordered various supplies 'to be delivered to Dr Oram's residence,' Tilly introduced herself and they exchanged brief pleasantries. Happening to meet in the same place again a few days later, they left the store together and strolled companionably up the street towards their adjacent houses.

'This wouldn't be done in England, would it?' said Isabella. 'A lady like you walking along in public with someone else's servant.'

'Things certainly tend to be less formal out here in the colony. The classes are closer together, and people don't stand on ceremony so strictly. I prefer it this way. Does it make you uncomfortable?'

'Not uncomfortable. But I'm a little unsure of what's considered proper in my position. Of course I understand that the Oram household needs to operate on a principle of decorum, but how to apply that in particular circumstances isn't quite clear to me yet.'

'It soon will be. By the way, Miss Trent, something in your voice suggests you probably hail from the Midlands – am I right?' Tilly ventured.

'Is it so obvious? Yes, I grew up in Staffordshire. My home town is at the edge of the moorlands. Or was; I suppose I must learn to regard this part of Australia as my home now.' She gave a rueful smile.

Occasionally in the following weeks they found opportunities for further conversation, increasingly relaxed in tone; and although Isabella steered away from any topic that might have touched on her reasons for coming to this country, it seemed to Tilly that the younger woman was beginning to find her feet here.

And then, like a jag of lightning suddenly splitting what had seemed a placid sky, came the terrible incident that would utterly change Isabella's life. Tilly would never forget things she saw and heard that day.

Leek
and
London
1880-87

FOUR

OOKING BACK IN LATER YEARS, LUCY MALPASS WOULD recognise this encounter as a turning point from which she began to move towards an unforeseen destination. But as yet she had no inkling of how such moments could change the course of one's life without announcing themselves as pivotal. For the time being, uppermost in her mind was merely a mild curiosity.

'There's nobody else quite like him,' Elizabeth Wardle told her. 'A truly exceptional man, as you'll soon see for yourself.' With a preening fingertip she adjusted slightly the tilt of her muslin cap, patting its blond lace trim and amber-hued ribbon.

'What should I expect, then?' asked Lucy.

Mrs Wardle puffed her plump cheeks and widened her eyes theatrically to signal that Lucy would be encountering prodigious qualities.

'He's a veritable human whirlwind, Mr Morris is. Whenever he comes to Leek he stays with us as a houseguest, and we've always had to brace ourselves lest we lose our footing, so to speak. The moment he arrives, a great gust of energy seems to blow open all the doors and rattle the casements.'

Chuckling, she wagged her head as if picturing one of these genial disturbances.

'Ideas tumble out of him,' she continued, 'tripping over each other. Questions, schemes, demands, opinions. He'll seize suddenly on some notion, and won't rest until he's turned it inside out and upside down and given it a thorough shaking. His friends call him Topsy, and I used to suppose this was because whatever he touches will soon turn topsy-turvy, though really the disorder is only temporary, a prelude to creating something that's orderly in a beautiful new way. My husband's cousin George, who works for him in London, says the nickname just refers to his famously dishevelled appearance: you'd think his hair had never known a comb, and this reminded someone of the character called Topsy in *Uncle Tom's Cabin*.'

'He sounds formidable. Like a big steam engine, is he?'

'More often he's just a kettle whistling merrily on the hob. Has a homely side to him, Mr Morris does. His occasional frowns don't mean much. It's a cheery heart he has. So no need to be apprehensive, Lucy.'

Apprehensive? No – that wasn't quite what Lucy felt. Certainly there was a tingle of excitement at the prospect of coming face to face with this remarkably versatile artist, renowned far and wide not only for his poetry but also for brilliant designs that animated so many kinds of material, from textiles to wallpapers, stained glass and furniture. A further thing put her on her mettle: the fact that he himself had asked to meet her after seeing the quality of the work she had done for the Leek Embroidery Society.

'He's been admiring in particular that portière you stitched so delicately in coloured silks,' Elizabeth Wardle reported. 'Finer than anything comparable in his Oxford Street showroom –

that's what he said, quite emphatically. Wanted to know how you'd learned such skill with a needle, and was astounded when I told him how young you are.'

So here she was now, waiting to be introduced. She knew he had gone early that morning with Mr Wardle to the Hencroft Works, and their return was overdue, midday having come and gone.

'What keeps them so long, do you think?' asked Lucy.

'Not hard to guess. Mr Morris is very particular about the colour of fabrics dyed for him here and sent to London, and when he isn't entirely satisfied he never hesitates to let my poor Thomas know. There's been a problem, he thinks, about inconsistent colours, and that's the main reason for his latest visit to Leek. I suppose he'll be up to his elbows in our vats right now, talking loudly to himself or to anyone within earshot. Upbraiding Thomas, no doubt.'

'A stickler for getting everything perfect?'

'Oh, indeed. It's been like that since he first spent time here, some five years ago. Meticulous. Demands the highest standards, and doesn't hold back on criticism. I still remember how he once offended one of Thomas's workmen, admittedly a clumsy fellow, by saying he had a "hippopotamus thumb"! But to be fair, he's no less exacting in his self-judgments. He's done his utmost to learn every little detail about dyeing textiles in natural colours – indigo, walnut, madder, weld and others. Not just to watch it being done, but to do as much as possible himself, and be candid about his shortcomings, and drive himself to improve. The aim is always to master it all with his own hands. And as I say that, I can still see him standing here in our doorway on one occasion, about to walk to the rail station for his journey home at the end of a visit: he was spreading his hands wide, grinning like a naughty schoolboy as he looked at the indelible dark blue stains on them, and joking that he'd now be utterly shunned by polite society back in London.'

They heard the boom of male voices coming up St Edward Street and approaching the front door. Loud expostulation, vigorous rejoinder, ebullient laughter. Then the clomp of boots along the hall.

Thomas Wardle entered the room first, adopting a contrite expression. 'Forgive us, my dear, I know we're later than expected but there were difficult matters to resolve.'

'My fault, Mrs Wardle, all my fault,' interjected the other man, portly and rumpled. 'I do apologise. Simply lost track of time, pursuing a more reliable method of fixing some of the dyes. Ah!' – as he caught sight of Lucy – 'You must be Miss Malpass! Delighted to meet you. Your needlework is quite splendid, quite splendid. A credit to Mrs Wardle's tutelage!'

The older woman made a gesture of modest demurral. 'I can't claim to have taught her much,' she said benignly. 'Lucy has a rare God-given talent. Our Leek Embroidery Society is lucky to have such a clever member. The other ladies are all competent in following the designs you've provided, Mr Morris, but only Lucy has such an aptitude for these tasks that she can readily devise her own ingenious variations.'

'And can execute them perfectly,' added Morris, beaming, 'to judge from the fine examples you showed me.' Glancing across at him, Lucy acknowledged his jovial smile with a grateful nod.

At the Wardles' long oak dinner table, where she and William Morris sat side by side as guests, it became clear to Lucy that it was not just in order to praise her work that this redoubtable visitor had sought to meet her.

As the food came and went, he bubbled with enthusiasm for what he called 'a spirited revival of traditional arts and crafts' across the nation and spoke generously of the high standard already achieved by Mrs Wardle and her disciples in the few months since the Leek Embroidery Society came into being. Beating the air with an emphatic fork, he declared it was now time to develop a closer connection between this promising regional enterprise and his own London-based firm.

'And what better way to do this' – turning here to Lucy – 'than to have you, Miss Malpass, working alongside us in the city?'

Startled, she looked at him uncertainly. 'Do you mean…?'

'I mean, to put it plainly, that we would all benefit if you were to move to London in the near future. I've raised this possibility with Mr and Mrs Wardle, who agree that, though your exemplary contribution here in Leek would of course be sorely missed, you have much to gain now by pursuing the refinement of your craft skills in a more…what shall I say? – a more intensely stimulating environment.' His fingers combed his thick beard.

'In London,' he went on expansively, 'there are ample opportunities to learn first-hand from some of England's finest artists and designers. I'm told you like to stand on your own feet. To be open to new ideas. Well, you could deepen your knowledge of textile decoration by frequenting the South Kensington Museum. Superb displays there! And you could combine study with paid employment at the Royal School of Art Needlework, guided by experienced teachers.'

'What's more,' said Thomas Wardle, leaning forward to endorse the idea, 'it would be a pleasantly efficient way, as Mr Morris has remarked, of fortifying the bond between his company and our own. Both of us have plans to expand, and we want to work more closely together. We'd value the help you could give by interpreting each to the other.'

Lucy raised her eyebrows. 'A go-between?'

'If you like to call it that,' said Morris, waving a hand airily and radiating amiable warmth.

She dabbed her mouth slowly with her napkin while shaping a reply. 'Moving away from Leek at this stage? I'm not averse to it, not at all, but…well, I've no very clear idea of what life in London might mean for a young single woman. Besides, I can't imagine that Mrs Brodie, my widowed aunt, would think it proper for me to travel alone to a distant city – far less to reside there without protective company. She's been watching over me dutifully ever since my parents died, and although she says I should feel free to choose my own path when the right time comes, I doubt she'd regard me as ready for this kind of independence. Not nearly.'

As Lucy was speaking, Elizabeth Wardle gave quick little nods of understanding. 'Barbara Brodie is quite right, of course, to be mindful of your welfare,' she said, still nodding like a fubsy pigeon. 'Even if you were several years older it would be irresponsible to let you move to London without a chaperone. But isn't it likely that she herself would willingly accompany you? There's nothing, as far as I can see, to keep her in Leek for the next few years. She could easily find tenants for her house.'

'And if we could persuade her,' added Thomas Wardle, 'that this is a great chance for you to develop your craft skills and gain due recognition, she wouldn't want to stand in your way, would she?'

Morris thwacked himself on the knee to signal reinforcement of the message. 'Now, Miss Malpass, you said you can't quite envisage what life in London would mean for you. Well, I'll tell you this: most assuredly, it need not mean being alone. My family would gladly look after your wellbeing, you can be certain of that. You'd be a welcome visitor at our home in Hammersmith, whenever you might wish for company. There you'd often meet a lively assortment of artists and designers and writers and thinkers. My daughter May, who's about your age and shares your passion for embroidery, would be keen to befriend you.'

'You're very kind, Mr Morris. Still, being not yet nineteen and familiar only with small-town country ways, I suppose it would take me quite some while to find my bearings in such a huge metropolis, and begin to feel comfortable there.'

'But you shouldn't feel overwhelmed by that thought, my dear. It's not as if you'd be confined to the city. From time to time my family likes to withdraw to our little country retreat, and you could spend time with us there occasionally. It's a quiet place in a rustic Oxfordshire village, Kelmscott. I'm not really an urban creature myself, you know. I prefer unspoiled landscapes, orchards, gardens, rivers. Rambling over the meadows. Riding my Mouse around the countryside…'

'Mouse?' Lucy's obvious confusion halted Morris's rush of words.

'Ah!' he said. 'I should explain. That's the name of a dwarf pony I brought back from Iceland a few years ago. Adorable little beast. Anyhow… My habitat, the place where my mind feels most at home, is the natural world, not the city. After all, a fundamental aim of our whole design movement is to adapt the patterns devised by nature – the forms of flowers, plants, twisting vines, birds… To recreate their vitality within the domestic interiors of everyday living. But on the other hand, only a large city can bring together a great energetic diversity of different people and ideas and activities…'

Mopping his forehead with a large red handkerchief, he looked at her enquiringly.

'I'll talk it over with my aunt,' said Lucy. 'But I'm sure she wouldn't let me live unchaperoned in London. So unless she's willing to go there with me, the plan hardly seems feasible.'

On a stilly morning in March 1881, the frost not yet gone from the railway platform, Lucy waited with Aunt Barbara to begin their journey, wishing she owned thicker-lined gloves and boots. Elizabeth Wardle had come to the station to bid them farewell. A kind gesture, thought Lucy, but the train was now overdue and conversation had dwindled; at a time like this there was little to be said. Their breath clung in small clouds of silence. Lucy felt impatient to get aboard, turn her back on Leek, and sink luxuriously into a prospective daydream.

At last the hissing huffing engine arrived, the tearful goodbyes were said, and the pair of travellers settled into their seats. As the countryside slipped past outside her compartment window there was a gradual shift in Lucy's mood, a dawning sense that it might be less easy to detach herself from this corner of north-eastern Staffordshire than she had supposed.

Turning her attention away from the window, Lucy glanced at her aunt. Barbara Brodie seemed to be gently stifling a smile, probably conscious of subtle ironies in the situation but disinclined to display her awareness of them. This was a countenance her aunt often wore, with a faint crinkle at the corners of her mouth and eyes hinting at thoughts that needn't be expressed. No wry mockery in it, just a restrained amusement at being able to see both ways. Little escaped her notice. In later years, long after the brutal incident that would suddenly change Aunt Barbara into a different person, Lucy would still picture her in this present attitude, discreetly watchful, as if pausing in some doorway of discernment, tilting her head appraisingly in one direction and then in another, looking into a room and out beyond it as well.

Having her aunt's companionship made this London venture seem less daunting. The business of finding suitable lodgings and installing themselves there with the help of their maid Elsie Perkins promised to be comparatively straightforward. As soon as they had moved from hotel accommodation to their new address, Perkins would follow with assorted portmanteau luggage, a medley of hatboxes and miscellaneous chattels. Yet the larger challenge of becoming accustomed little by little to the ways of the urban world would take some time, and though the ideal of self-reliance appealed to Lucy she knew she was not yet fully equipped to achieve it. Living in Barbara Brodie's comfortably familiar home for nearly six years, taking much for granted, she had leant on her sole relative's considerate support and tactful guidance in many practical matters. While seldom expressing disapproval, Aunt Barbara managed to exert a moderating influence by way of occasional gentle remarks about her niece's tendency to swing between the cautious and the impulsive. Elizabeth Wardle, too, had been somewhat like a mother to her: more than just an exemplar of excellence in craftwork, she had nurtured Lucy's own ambition to excel. Would that ambition now prove capable of thriving independently? She would miss, as well, the companionship of fellow members of the Leek Embroidery Society. Though none of them occupied a central place in her affections or shared her zealous devotion to a creative calling, there was a bond in the knowledge that together they had enlisted their skills in a worthy common cause, working to restore ornamental needlework to the high status it once enjoyed among the decorative arts. From large altar frontals for local churches to a variety of domestic pieces sold through the Wardles' shop, the work of the Society had quickly established a standard of artistry much admired not only in Staffordshire but also as far away as London.

A pang of retrograde sentiment gripped her. The people she was leaving behind belonged to a very particular place, a cherished place, which hitherto had been her only home. Her selfhood was almost inseparable from everything that constituted Leek and its vicinity: the wide sloping streets, the mills and chapels, the silk factories and dyeworks, the bustling crowds and noisy cattle thronging the markets on Wednesdays, the way the modest ancient buildings and the proud new ones nestled into the hillside, all of that and more was now receding, and the thought struck her that she might never see it again.

At Stoke-on-Trent they changed trains. Never before had she ventured this far. Now, as she moved further and further away from Leek, scenes surrounding her home township lingered behind her eyes, a private store of images, especially of the dark-furrowed moorlands with their great outcropping cloud-nudging rocks and the glint of winter snow on craggy ramparts of the Roaches, highest part of the curving gritstone ridge whose southern edge was Hen Cloud with its steep-sloping scarp. Her train rattled on southwards. In a kind of trance, Lucy pictured fondly the famous double sunset, a natural wonder that brought sightseers to Leek in midsummer so that they could stand in the churchyard and watch the sun setting on the summit of Hen Cloud before partly reappearing and then setting for a second time at the base of the hill – a temporary resurrection followed by the final descent into darkness, as if foreboding had over-shadowed hope.

FIVE

—

$\mathcal{R}$AIL JOURNEYS, LUCY SOON DISCOVERED, WERE BY NO means all alike. The one that had carried her so joltingly from Leek to London in her aunt's company took many long hours, filled not only with clatter and clank and sooty smoke but also with countless changes of patterned colour as towns, hamlets, hedgerows, open fields, river valleys and wooded hillsides rolled slowly past her window in the shifting light. Now, just three weeks later, she was embarking on a quite different excursion with a quite different companion. A short ride, this one, devoid of scenic views: she would be travelling for the first time on an underground line. Atingle with curiosity, she boarded the train at Kensington High Street station, gently guided by May Morris. Fragments of breakfast scone and marmalade moved queasily in her stomach. She should not have had that second cup of tea.

Although they chose a first-class carriage, its warm air was foul. All windows were kept closed because the engine had to discharge steam into the tunnel, but the acrid reek of sulphur and coal dust still penetrated their compartment, mingling with fumes from the oil lamp above and with pipe exhalations from the male passengers.

'Ugh. I feel nearly suffocated,' whispered Lucy.

'That's the price of convenient transportation,' May replied with a shrug, 'not that the street air above is much better. But yes, it's noisome down here, indeed. My father detests the underground railway. He likes to describe it as "a vapour-bath of hurried and discontented humanity." Always the phrase-maker.' Her grin was warmly indulgent.

Getting off at Sloane Square, they shooed away some flapping pigeons and walked up Sloane Street towards the Royal School of Art Needlework. The thoroughfare was crowded, clamorous, full of bustle. At times they could hardly hear themselves speak above the strident yelling of street urchins and birdseed hawkers, the rumbling of carriage wheels, the whinnying and clomping of horses, and resounding cheers from the nearby Prince's Club, where the new fad known as lawn tennis was attracting large crowds.

Lucy's enrolment formalities at the Royal School of Art Needlework proceeded expeditiously, smoothed by letters of recommendation from Elizabeth Wardle and William Morris as well as by May's self-confident presence at her elbow. Forms were signed, instructions imparted, practical arrangements made. Within half an hour the two young women emerged again into the hubbub of the thronged street.

'Nothing too daunting about that little journey, was there?' May asked as they strolled together back towards the station. 'And remember,' she added, 'much of the time I'll be nearby, attending classes at the School of Design. So we can often meet up on weekdays. Besides, you'll always be a welcome guest in our family home, you know that. Evenings and Sundays we usually have lively company there.'

Lucy nodded gratefully. Their friendship seemed to have been instantaneous, effortless. Based on mutual recognition of each other's quick intelligence and love of artful design, it was reinforced by the fortuity that they were also, as it transpired, exact coevals. Looking over Lucy's shoulder during her enrolment process, May had exclaimed at one of the registered details: 'Twenty-fifth of March 1862 – that's my own birth date, too!'

'Twins, then.'

'Though not in appearance.' They inspected each other quizzically, laughing at the physical contrast. Lucy's hair was wheat-coloured, May's dark. Lucy's eyes were grey-green, May's a gleaming brown. Lucy's features had the pale aspect and delicate symmetry of traditional Saxon fairness, while May's olive skin and prominent nose and chin lent her a gypsy allure. Lucy's medium height seemed short beside May's tall stature, to which an unusually long neck gave emphasis.

'Chalk and cheese,' said May.

'Hmm. But those objects don't complement each other at all,' said Lucy, shaking her head. 'I'd prefer to think of us as warp and weft.'

Smiling, they parted company at the station.

'Now that you're familiar with the underground,' May had assured her, 'you'll find it a simple matter to travel alone to and from the Art Needlework School. These days it's perfectly respectable for an unescorted woman to use the railway, and quite safe.'

Yet in fact there was no guarantee of safety, as Lucy found a fortnight later. Halfway between stations on the Metropolitan Line, the only woman in a tight-packed compartment, she became aware of a muttering sound to her left. From the corner of her eye she could see a thickset man leaning forward in his seat, head bobbing and jowls quivering as he spoke to himself in unintelligible phrases. Then he stood up, hitched his trousers, hitched them again, moved in front of Lucy and raised his index finger. Pointing at her and grinning foolishly, he began to chuckle in a coarse guttural way. Spittle fell from his lower lip. He was, she saw, quite mad. Dangerous? Perhaps. She looked away. Suddenly reaching forward, he tugged her sleeve. Incensed, she lifted her umbrella and struck his forearm as hard as she could. With a yelp he staggered backwards to his window seat, wincing as he rubbed the flesh above his wrist. All the other men in the compartment, half a dozen of them, remained frozen to their seats.

She glared across at her assailant, who seemed now to have sunk back into his private demented thoughts. There must be countless lunatics wandering around London, she thought, far outnumbering the crazed wretches held in Bethlem. Inevitably, from time to time, some of these stray madmen would find their way into railway carriages, where a few might become violent and menace people without warning. One couldn't rely on male passengers to act swiftly in that kind of emergency, Lucy saw, looking disdainfully around her compartment as the train came to a stop at Sloane Square and she rose to disembark. Behind their bristly beards and stern suits they were milksops, all of them.

Turning the corner into her street as the afternoon light began to fade, Lucy glanced along at the series of five-storey terrace houses and felt again a twitch of distaste at the humdrum style of their construction. The fourth-floor flat that she and her aunt had decided to rent was quite spacious, well appointed, and agreeably situated. Extending south from Kensington Road, close to the Albert Memorial in one direction and an underground rail station in the other, De Vere Gardens had a prosperous air and a convenient position. Yet despite its bid for handsomeness the street, in her eyes, lacked distinction. Created only a few years previously as a speculative development on the site of a former hippodrome and associated stables, it beckoned upper middle-class buyers with an array of substantial villas featuring white Suffolk bricks, Portland stone facades, red granite portico columns, canted bay windows and decorative balcony railings. Lucy thought these buildings staid at best, verging on pomposity. It did not surprise her that the market for which they were intended turned out to be smaller than the developers hoped. A few of the houses, including what was now her own address, had reportedly remained empty for more than two years before being converted into mansion blocks of tenanted apartments.

During the previous decade this once-verdant district had been quickly absorbed into London's spreading grey contagion. Roads and railways subdued the last remnants of green fields; soot began to coat the surviving trees and bushes; sunlight grew wan. Before long these pretentious Kensington dwellings would become grimy, and even in their transitory newness they were plainly inferior, Lucy thought, to the quality of the best domestic structures back in Leek. Her inward eye could recall the details of several redbrick homes around her town, designed by Leek's foremost local architects, the Sugdens; relatively modest in scale, using simple materials and restrained decoration, those familiar houses were harmonious in form – unlike the De Vere Gardens properties, which strained to impose themselves in an obtrusively masculine way, juxtaposing different features rather than integrating them.

Irritation gripped her at the thought that men generally claimed exclusive control of design in the public sphere. Architecture, like engineering and even landscape gardening, was their uncontested preserve; male notions about taste, proportion and materials shaped almost every modern urban building. The disposition of many interior spaces, too, and the furnishing of them, reflected primarily what men presumed to deem suitable.

One reason why Mr Morris's ideas attracted her so strongly was that his radical way of considering design questions, questions about built forms and the things they framed, was respectfully attentive to the knowledge and preferences of women as well as of men. May had told her that he encouraged his wife, daughters and sister-in-law to be forthright in expressing what they thought of textile patterns, of the balance of colours, of the best way to combine different fabrics and other substances. And although May had been a mere infant when the family's bespoke Red House was sold, her parents so often talked about it that it continued to embody in her imagination an ideal of domestic design, harking back to medieval traditions of building. Listening to May's description of some of its features – the exposed brickwork chimneypieces, the disregard for specious symmetries, the handcrafted motifs – Lucy was reminded of the Sugdens' buildings in Leek.

Having been warmly received as a frequent visitor in the Morris household, she had spent enough time there by now to recognise the whole family's steady resolve to resist any assumption that the field of design belonged to men. Of course 'Old Father William,' as May called him in her irreverent but fond way, still tended to dominate conversations with his high spirits, voicing opinions vehemently, but when he spoke of the need for arts and crafts to develop in the light of women's ideas as well as men's there was no doubting his sincerity or the particular confidence he placed in May's talents.

Strongly encouraged by her father, May was one of the few women attending the School of Design in South Kensington, where one could receive training in the practical arts, applicable to manufacturing and other branches of industry. While its main purpose remained the preparation of young men for teaching posts, it made room for 'exceptionally capable ladies.' When May talked about her classes at the School of Design and the ample scope they gave to individual creativity, Lucy felt a passing twinge of envy, conscious that the long hours she herself was spending at the Royal School of Art Needlework – grandly named, but just a little room above a bonnet shop – must be confined almost entirely to executing other people's designs. Yet despite the constraint she found a modicum of satisfaction in this because of the tactile and visual subtleties of all the different fabrics and threads that she was learning to handle more delicately, more precisely, from linen embroidered with wools to felted cloth embroidered with silks. She relished the challenge of increasing her dexterity in using various stitches: laid and couched, stem and satin, darning and speckling...so much close work, so many techniques to deploy, so many fine adjustments to make, so many miniscule choices to ponder. Her accomplished teachers included Mrs Morris's sister, Elizabeth Burden, whose skilful revival and adaptation of cushion stitching was greatly admired. Besides, Lucy and her fellow students had many splendid patterns to work from. Some were supplied by William Morris himself, no less. Some, incorporating large repetitive motifs, drew on traditional Eastern and Italian woven silks displayed in the

South Kensington Museum. Lucy's world shimmered with bright hues and fine tints, with inventive shapes and diverse textures. She revelled in the richness of it, though also feeling circumscribed.

'You don't tell me much about this Art Needlework School of yours,' said her aunt in their drawing room one evening. They both put aside their novels: Barbara Brodie had been dipping into Mrs Oliphant's *Squire Arden* while Lucy was engrossed in George Eliot's *The Mill on the Floss*, trying to decide whether Maggie Tulliver deserved sympathy or a smart slap. 'Do you like it there? Does it provide what you'd hoped for?'

'Oh, it's generally pleasant enough,' Lucy replied. 'And yes: though the tasks are seldom exciting, I've learnt to use a greater variety of stitching methods. I must say the women there are perfectly friendly, though I'm conscious that my situation and purpose are different from theirs, in the main. Most of my fellow students need the income that their labour brings, modest as it is. Some of them, I would guess, are in quite straitened circumstances, so they often take away additional pieces of work to embroider in their own time. Menial tasks to eke out their earnings. I'm fortunate in not feeling that financial pressure – in being able to explore the most demanding designs, the artistry of them, and to improve my skills in an unhurried way.'

'I'm glad to hear it. Nevertheless,' said Aunt Barbara, 'I have an impression, my dear, that you're not entirely contented with your classes there. I don't see any flush of enthusiasm on your cheek these days, except when you've returned from visiting the Morrises.'

'They're very kind to me, the Morris family. And I feel a special rapport with May, as you know. Her vivacity is contagious.'

'Isn't it also that their home is quite a magnet for other lively visitors? Good company, including a few young gentlemen?'

'I've met several interesting people there, certainly. Writers, artists, exuberant talkers.'

'Eligible bachelors?'

'Oh, please, Aunt!' Lucy flapped her hand irritably. 'Spare me your premature matchmaking thoughts.'

'Protest though you may, Lucy, you're at an age where it's surely natural to keep an eye open for a congenial companion. I thought there were deserving fellows in Leek whose advances you discouraged…'

'Deserving? Sheer dullards, all of them!'

'That's unduly severe, I think. In London, at any rate, there must be a good number of suitable…'

'Suitability is not an enticing quality. Not in my eyes.'

'I do wish you wouldn't scowl like that, Lucy. So disagreeable. I know you value your independence, and I admire you for it, but sooner or later you'll have to acknowledge that your future should involve a man.'

'Why?' she burst out. 'Why should it? And anyhow, why must I think about it now? I'm just nineteen. The only man who has ever been important to me was my father, and I'm in no hurry to let anyone displace him.' Pointedly she turned away and picked up her book again.

'You've always had a fiery spirit, Lucy. It burns more fiercely in you than in anyone else I know. Just take care that the flames don't scorch you and those near you.'

SIX

THE HEADY SOCIAL PLEASURES OF TIME SPENT WITH THE Morrises absorbed Lucy's attention with such immediacy that it would be a long while before she saw how subtly this family's passionate interests were also shaping the cache of imagery that fed her inner life and foretold its eventual curtailment.

Through the filtering elm leaves, on through the south-facing windows, flecks of river-rippled light came glittering towards her and skipped across the long drawing room. In mid-conversation she glanced about as the sunbeams flickered over her surroundings. An azure carpet embellished with strips of oriental rugs. Large brocaded hangings on the pictureless walls. A row of ornamental plates above the fireplace. Sparse furniture: a few adjustable armchairs, the painted settle on which both women were resting, and little else. In this uncluttered space she felt calm, yet with a quickening of the senses.

'Taking you under our wing?' May raised an amused eyebrow. 'That's not how we think of it. You're perfectly self-reliant, Lucy. We wouldn't presume to coddle and cosset you.'

'All the same, I'm grateful for the way you've all drawn me so cordially into your circle.'

'We like your company. When you visit us you brighten the room.'

'No no, it's the other way round. Being here with you and the family circle makes me feel I'm borrowing some luminous quality from your household.'

'Well, let's not quibble over a figure of speech. I'm glad you enjoy spending time with us despite our foibles. Some people find us a rather peculiar flock, you know. Gregarious to the point of seeming oppressive. Probably you've been accustomed to a more placid home life.'

'Yes, much quieter, living with my aunt, though I did spend a good deal of time in the Wardles' house, and it was always abuzz with commotion. Not just their eight spirited children and several servants but the continual comings and goings too, what with Mr Wardle's business affairs and Mrs Wardle's embroidery school and all their church activities. Often on the verge of becoming disorderly, yet somehow they held it all together.'

'How long have you been with your aunt?'

'Since my father died. About six years.'

'What of your mother?'

'I hardly remember her. I was just an infant when something went dreadfully wrong with the birth of a second baby and carried them both off. So my upbringing was in my father's hands. Just the two of us, not counting our cook and housemaid.'

'And then at the time of his death you were still hardly more than a child. That must have been terrible.'

'Oh it was, May. Indescribably distressing. The suddenness. He rode off after breakfast, waving to me cheerfully, and before noon there were two men at our door telling me they'd found him lifeless at the roadside, thrown by his horse.' Lucy closed her eyes for a moment and drew in a long breath before continuing.

'I felt at the time that it was my fault, that he wouldn't have died but for a whim of mine.' She paused again, and May looked at her enquiringly.

'Why was that?'

'The accident happened about three miles south of Leek, in the Churnet Valley, when he was on his way to look at an abandoned factory, the Cheddleton Silk Mill, with a view to buying it – something I'd been imploring him to do for months, after he'd taken me there for a picnic outing. It was such a tranquil, picturesque spot between the river and the canal, beside a little bridge and a cluster of industrial buildings – the tall silk mill with its solid stone base topped by brick upper storeys and a chimney stack, the brewery nearby and the pair of flint mills with their massive waterwheels. A girlish notion came to me: my father, I fancied, could extend his silk manufacturing business by simply acquiring this old empty mill and getting it back into working order. Of course I knew nothing about whether such a scheme was commercially feasible, but he said it merited some thought, perhaps just humouring me at first, and then he began to regard it as a serious possibility. So that fatal ride down the valley... He intended to inspect the condition of equipment – spindles, looms, steam engine – that had been standing idle in the mill for years.'

'What was he like, your father?'

Lucy bit her lip. The truth was too difficult to put fully into words, and she veered away from some of it. 'A wounded soul, I think,' she said, her voice low. 'The way my mother had died, taking with her a stillborn baby who would have become his son: it left a kind of hidden hurt curling inside him, unacknowledged. So he could sometimes be withdrawn, austere, and yet he was my dearest companion and I loved him deeply.'

She was going to add, 'He casts a troubling shadow over any other man.' Left it unsaid. Let her thought slink beneath their conversation like a sinuous undercurrent while May spoke.

'Although I haven't known family bereavement, I can share some of your feelings. You've seen how close I am to my own father, despite his blemishes and quirks.'

'An enviable relationship,' said Lucy. 'And he's an admirable man.' But yes, she thought, very much the eccentric, often strange in his language and behaviour. Strange in appearance, too, with his wild hair and unruly whiskers: he looked like a hasty sketch of a windswept haystack. Those unkind comic drawings of him by Mr Burne-Jones, distributed and chuckled over within their circle, were only slight exaggerations of the amusing figure that he often cut. Yet it was this unkempt, sometimes clumsy man who devised and meticulously produced so many exquisite textile designs, peerless in their delicacy. When she first saw his cele-brated acanthus pattern on a sample in the Oxford Street shop of Morris and Co. it had struck her like a revelation, and she stood in front of it for a long while, staring, lost in a daydream of wonder-ment. The perfectly balanced tinting, an equipoise of sage-green and russet and pale lemon, lustrous as a sunlit flowerbed. The witty interplay of those curlicue shapes, flamelike branchings and gently geometric borders. The consummate skill of its fine needlecraft and knotwork, embellishing the cotton so adroitly with silk and satin threads. It seemed miraculous that this composition, along with many others of breathtaking brilliance, had come from the head and hand of such an unprepossessing oddity.

William Morris's ground-floor study, Lucy found, was very different in character from the drawing room above it. Puritanically plain, lacking any curtains or carpet, it was unfurnished except for bookshelves, a small loom, a trestle table and a couple of chairs.

'Ah! Miss Malpass! Come in, come in! Here's the thing I wanted to show you. Do look at this. It's one of the first publications of the Early English Text Society: *Sir Gawayne and the Green Knight*. A wonderful poem, rescued from obscurity by scholarly labour.'

The book lay open on the table. Morris slowly turned its pages, a delighted expression on his shining face. 'Such richness in the language!' he declared. 'It transports me utterly, you know. Transports me across the centuries into a magnificent medieval world. This old courtly tale of questing and testing has a powerful momentum that carries readers along, but there's so much detail to relish as well.'

'What kind of detail?'

'In the texture of its language! What appeals to me especially is the way the poem keeps lingering sensuously over descriptions of gorgeous garments, drapes, tapestries, counterpanes. Like a sample book displaying swatches of different fabrics. On page after page there's a profusion of silk on show: Guinevere's dais is covered with a silk canopy, Gawain stands on a luxurious red silk carpet to don his armour, exotic silk tapestries hang on the bedroom walls of Sir Bertilak's castle. The poet mentions other sorts of cloth as well, table linen, a velvet coat and so on. And the lines glow with colour! Blues and browns, whites and reds, greens and golds.'

He kept turning the pages, murmuring to himself and then picking up the thread of conversation again. 'Often there's an emphasis on elegant needlework. Both the Green Knight and Gawain have birds and flowers sewn on their clothing. See this word here, "enbrawden" – embroidered: it recurs many times. As I read, my fingers can almost fondle the fabrics, the ornamental stitches…'

He's like a fountain, Lucy thought, a brimming fountain of childlike rapture.

He flowed on.

'And another thing, young lady, will interest you about this ancient poem: there's a sprinkle of dialect words bearing the distinctive marks of your very own home region! Just before you came in I was going over these lines, look, at the beginning of Part 4, evoking stormy weather, and it struck me that the phrase used here for the driven snow, *snitered ful snart* – I've heard it myself in Leek, and nowhere else. You know the expression, probably?'

'I do, yes. I can hear the phrase in our cook's mouth. It means *the snow swirled, piercingly cold* – doesn't it?'

'Exactly. And the words belong to your part of the country. To most Londoners they'd be meaningless. There are other fragments, too, of your local language scattered through *Sir Gawain*. I believe it was written somewhere close to Leek, and not only because of its traces of dialect.'

His eyes were sparkling excitedly, and she smiled back as he went on with contagious zest. 'Another clue to its origin, you see, is that features of the poem's landscape resemble particular places in that corner of Staffordshire. I'm sure the author had firsthand knowledge of the moorland wastes near the edge of the Peak. Lud's Church, for instance, that huge mossy cleft in a hillside just a few miles north from your town: I've walked up there with Wardle and I can tell you the description of the Green Chapel in this text matches it precisely!'

'I'm no scholar,' said Lucy, 'but I can see it gives you great pleasure, being able to make sense of something written so very long ago. Enviable.'

'Great pleasure indeed.'

Morris fell silent for a moment, looking puzzled and abstracted. He put his hand to his forehead. 'But I've got carried away by the Gawain story. Wasn't there something else I said I wanted to show you? I've forgotten.'

'You invited me to see a few things you brought back from your trips to Iceland.'

'Ah yes, yes. My little collection. I keep most of the pieces in this cabinet.'

Clearing a space on the trestle table, he pulled miscellaneous items from small boxes and laid them out lovingly for her to inspect. There were articles of decorative clothing: a cap, a pair of slippers, an embroidered bodice, a corded sash, a girdle, a woven belt. He lifted each in turn, pointing out various details. There were also cooking utensils, drinking vessels, and a carved horn container capped with brass and etched with an intricate design of flowers and sinuous leafage. Then he placed before her a sixteenth-century Bible, opening it to reveal an array of Norse words.

'How strange Iceland's language looks,' she murmured. 'Though not to you, of course. I know you've made a study of it, and translated some of the sagas.'

'I have, I have. With the indispensable teacherly help of my friend Magnusson.'

'Painstaking work, I suppose.' *I ought to read some of his poetry*, she thought.

'A labour of love. But I remember now: in particular, what I had in mind to show you is the design reproduced in this drawing of mine, made in ink and watercolour when I was in Reykjavík. I copied meticulously a large old wall hanging. It had a linen surface entirely covered with long-armed cross stitches, creating a ground in plain weave. I think I've made a good fist of capturing that texture, as well as the way it was embroidered with strands of bright silk and variegated woollen yarns. Here, look: an amazing composition, don't you think? Brilliant, in a weird manner.'

Leaning forward, Lucy stared in silent admiration at the interplay of pattern and palette, slowly sucking every part of it into her memory. The contrast of colours was striking: predominantly gold and red, with small flecks of white and a dark blue-green that was almost black. There were human and animal shapes, set within octagonal frames and surrounded by lozenges and layered borders.

'What an extraordinary design!' she said. 'Some of the motifs are puzzling, but the balance of it all is quite beautiful. Those horsemen, and the figures that seem to be dancing: does the way they're patterned tell a story of some kind, do you think?'

He shrugged. 'If so, it's very elusive.'

'To me the dancers look like mummers wearing animal masks. Their joined hands form a ring.'

He peered at the pattern. 'I think you're right. Very observant of you, Miss Malpass.'

In the middle of the encircling group there had evidently been a larger figure, most of which was missing. Lucy pointed to it enquiringly. 'It was a ragged hole in the fabric,' said Morris. 'Someone may have cut it out deliberately. A shame.'

'How big is the original work?'

'About as tall as you are.'

'You saw it on the wall of someone's house?'

'In one of the attics in Reykjavík where the National Museum of Iceland has stored its holdings. I'd met the museum's curator, Jón Árnason, who explained that many items in his country's precious collection had been transferred from Denmark just a few years earlier and there wasn't yet a proper building to house them in, so they'd been dispersed across the town. He took me from place to place, and when I saw this remarkable piece I begged him to let me copy it on paper. He was perfectly obliging, so I sat in front of it for hours with my pens and paints and brushes, trying to do justice to it.'

Lucy peered at the design more closely. 'There's something uncanny about those stiff figures. The disconcerting way they look out at us from their impassive faces. Is it doleful or menacing? Who are they, I wonder?'

'Quite mysterious, I agree. The whole thing seems to resist interpretation, and yet it's no less haunting for that. The boldly dyed fibres, the strong dark lines interwoven with primary hues... To my mind this clash of colours calls up the landscapes and skies of Iceland.' He closed his eyes. 'I remember fiery sunsets mingling flamboyantly with emerald northern lights. I remember sprinklings of delicate flowers – sea pink and bladder campion – among black lava rocks along the shoreline, as if a giant hand had spread out a magical Persian carpet. So much of the countryside seems utterly barren, and then these surprising flares of beauty dazzle your eyes. Startle your heart.'

Morris withdrew momentarily into a little private reverie before he spoke again.

'Iceland reduces everything to its essentials. I love the place for its harsh simplicity. It forces people to sustain themselves and each other – their souls as well as their bodies. Much of their sense of community comes from traditional craftwork, traditional customs. They're continually singing together, especially in groups of men, keeping the old stories and tunes alive. Families take great pride in weaving their own clothing and household fabrics. In the turf farmsteads I visited, a loom is the central piece of furniture.'

He shuffled across the room to his own small handloom and stood there patting it affectionately, as if it were his pony. He looked like a character in some old folk tale.

Years later, with this image of him beside his loom still clear in her mind, she would often recall their conversation, pensively turning over what he had told her about flashes of colour in the old Gawain poem and in the bleak wastes of Iceland. Above all, she held in her memory every particular of the richly embroidered wall hanging that he had so carefully copied with pen and brush. In time it would become an emblem of her destiny.

SEVEN

*I*N SLY DISGUISE, CATASTROPHE BIDED ITS TIME. MEANWHILE month after month passed in a pleasant haze and the anniversary of Lucy's move to London went by unnoticed.

One balmy Saturday afternoon during her second London summer, she and her aunt entered a hansom and were driven towards an address near Regents Park. It was the first warm dry weather for a fortnight, and almost the entire populace seemed to be out and about. Through the carriage window Lucy glimpsed an endless succession of other cabs trundling past, and leisurely throngs sauntering along every footpath.

She had no clear notion of what to expect from the social occasion that awaited them in Park Crescent. Their prospective hostess, Mrs Aurora Watson, a wealthy distant cousin of Aunt Barbara's late husband, was renowned for the elaborate afternoon teas, soirées and dance parties that she liked to arrange in her home. The invitation to today's event had mentioned 'a tea dance.' What would this involve? Aunt Barbara was vague on the subject, so Lucy had asked May about it, receiving a satirical answer. Ordinary little rituals of exchanging gossip over a sandwich or a cake, said May, had now become faddishly inflated by the idle rich into grand receptions featuring not only an ostentatious cornucopia of refreshments but also assorted activities such as piano recitals, vocal performances, card games and – more extravagantly – carpet dancing.

'Carpet dancing?'

'Cutting a caper on the Kidderminster. Have you done much dancing?'

'Just a little, in Leek. My aunt insisted that I learn a few of the standard routines, but I've no enthusiasm for that kind of thing.'

'I'm told a tea dance requires a zestful display. Ladies are required to frolic like frisky fillies. '

'Ugh! So the whole affair promises to be quite loathsome.'

On the contrary it turned out to be a pleasurable experience, and one that would have far-reaching consequences.

The moment they arrived, Aurora Watson greeted them affably and put them at their ease. Two maidservants were on hand to look after practical matters, taking care of their coats, indicating the tables of food and providing glasses of sherry with soda water. ('Tea is also served continuously in the back dining room, Madam, should you wish to partake at any time.')

'Presently I'll introduce you to some of the guests,' Mrs Watson told them, 'but one of the military officers, Julius Kendrick, is about to sing to us, so do take a seat in the drawing room. My daughter will provide the pianoforte accompaniment.'

Patting a wayward curl into place beneath her ear, Lucy went through the doorway with her aunt into the largest and most ornate domestic room she had ever seen. Rows of chairs faced the piano where a shy-looking young woman sat. No older than I am, Lucy thought. A tall barrel-chested man in a scarlet tunic crossed the room, took up a formal stance beside the piano and nodded to the accompanist. Then familiar phrases began to unfurl and swell.

Believe me, if all those endearing young charms
That I gaze on so fondly today
Were to fade by tomorrow and fleet in my arms...

Though this sentimental ditty was well known to most of the listeners, few until now had heard it rendered in such a honey-rich baritone. Its resonance disquieted Lucy. As the notes rose up and fell away in a recurrent rhythm, undulating from line to line, she was startled to feel this insistently masculine voice enter her body, seeming to vibrate through her bones. A faint internal shuddering alarmed her. The song continued to soar and subside, soar and subside, until it rolled on into the cadence of its final quatrain:

For the heart that has truly loved never forgets,
But as truly loves on to the close,
As the sunflower turns on her god, when he sets,
The same look which she turned when he rose.

Applause burst out around her. Lucy sat in rapt silence, immobile, her breath clenched in the back of her throat. Her aunt was talking to her – 'cuts a fine figure...admirable voice' – but she could only nod in response. And then Mrs Watson was sailing directly towards them with the debonair red-coated singer at her side.

'Ladies,' she said, 'I'd like to present Captain Kendrick. My Staffordshire cousin Mrs Brodie and her niece Miss Malpass.'

During the exchange of formal greetings, even when he bowed, Lucy had to tilt her head back to look him in the face. Her sudden tremor of diffidence annoyed her. Never before had she lacked poise in the presence of a man, but something about this soldier's self-possessed bearing flustered her. His eyes gleamed like burnished jet. She dropped her gaze, glancing sidelong at the dark beard, the broad shoulders, the large but well-proportioned hands.

'May I escort you to the tearoom, Miss Malpass?' Regaining her composure, she took his proffered arm and went through to the area where refreshments were laid out. His smile and gestures seemed smoothly practised. He's too sure of himself, she thought; he probably regards me as merely an opportunity for exercising his charm. Resistance stiffened in her. Yet despite herself she couldn't ignore the timbre of his voice. It compelled her receptive attention.

The prospect of dancing made her uneasy, bringing buried sensations near the surface of memory. She pushed away those obscure feelings from the past.

In a blurred sequence of waltzes, quadrilles, conversations, musical items and interludes for refreshment, afternoon slid imperceptibly into evening. Turning it all over in her mind as the carriage took her back with her aunt to their De Vere Gardens flat, Lucy was perturbed to find herself dwelling on physical details – the look and sound of him as they glided over the floor, the touch of his warm hands during the dances, the tang of masculinity. What exactly he had said to her was at first harder to recall; his conversation, like the little ballad he had sung, seemed less memorable for its content than for the sonorous tone of it. She could give only vague answers to her aunt's questions.

'Hmm? Oh yes, somewhere near Winchester, I believe he said. A place in the country.'

'What brings him to London, do you know?'

'He's on leave of some sort from his Hampshire Regiment. Staying at the Albany Street Barracks.'

'Just a brief visit, then?'

'I suppose so. His regiment will soon be off to somewhere in India.'

'While you were twirling around the room with him in the waltz, Mrs Watson told me a little about the Kendrick family. Landed gentry, very prosperous.'

'He didn't mention wealth.'

'I should think not. That would have been unmannerly.' Smiling to herself, Barbara Brodie inspected a button on one of her lavender gloves. 'I could see his good breeding in the way he holds himself. Quite a distinguished air, don't you think? Not stiff, like some military men. A nimble-footed dancer, for such a tall and muscular man.'

Lucy gave a little shrug. 'The polish comes from practice, no doubt. He said something about tea dances being popular in garrison towns. I didn't pay close attention to his chitchat.'

Her aunt looked at her quizzically. 'I'm sure this nonchalant attitude towards Captain Kendrick is a pretence, Lucy. I do hope you won't treat him with affected indifference when he calls here to see us on Sunday. You heard how warmly he responded to my invitation.'

'I'm perfectly capable of being civil to a visitor, Aunt Barbara. But I can read your thoughts. Please don't start scheming to marry me off.'

'My dear, you could do much worse than become part of the Kendrick family.'

'Pfff! Can you really see me in the role of a soldier's wife? Languishing in some regimental barracks? Giving up my cherished embroidery work so that I can launder dirty shirts and darn moth holes in uniforms?'

Smiling, her aunt raised a hand in surrender. 'Just enjoy his company, then, while it's on hand. You said he'll be going overseas before long.'

The following Sunday afternoon their maidservant brought Kendrick's calling card to Mrs Brodie on a salver, and he was soon sitting with them, deftly drawing both women into light-hearted conversation. As they talked about the tea dance hosted with such verve by Mrs Watson, Lucy forgot her intention to remain slightly aloof. The spirited dancing, the lavish spread of food, the agreeable company – it had all been very pleasant, they agreed.

'And your singing, Captain, was for me the most memorable feature of the occasion,' said Barbara Brodie. 'You must have had some musical training, surely?'

'Only from my mother, whose encouragement was not uncritical. Music always seemed to be ringing through our house when I was young. Just as it does nowadays through our barrack room. Some of my fellow-officers sing lustily. Even gracefully, a few of them.'

'What you sing among yourselves,' said Lucy, 'is less maudlin, I imagine, than the parlour piece you chose last Saturday.'

Her aunt frowned at her. 'Maudlin? That's a harsh judgment,' she said.

'But not unfair,' said Kendrick disarmingly. 'And as for the mess hall's taste in music, you're partly correct, Miss Malpass. You'd be more likely to hear a booming ballad with a refrain that summons every available voice. But our soldier songs can be sentimental, nonetheless. Imagine half a battalion of us, throats made pliable by rum, waxing lugubrious to the strains of a dirge like *Wrap me up in my tarpaulin jacket.*' His laugh made her think of a cello.

Lucy remembered Morris's mention of Icelandic men singing earnestly together to ward off the winter darkness and affirm the things they shared. She could glimpse something oddly appealing in a cohesive masculine ritual of that sort. Nothing seemed comparable to it among women, in her experience, except for the quiet companionability of groups such as the Leek Embroidery Society and the Royal Art Needlework School.

Before taking his leave, Kendrick asked whether they would accompany him the following Sunday afternoon on a stroll in Kensington Gardens, weather permitting. He would like to bring a fellow-soldier with him: his close friend and foster-brother Lieutenant Barton. Without hesitation it was all agreed and arranged.

Their promenade took them along crowded pathways until they reached the Albert Memorial. They walked slowly around the grand edifice, Julius Kendrick at Lucy's side while behind them his friend Gerard Barton escorted her aunt. Kendrick admired the statuary, pointing to various details in the gilded bronze colossus of the late Prince Consort under its Gothic canopy and the scores of surrounding figures.

'Superb monument,' he said. 'Superb. Especially the effigy of Prince Albert, presiding over it all.' She noticed that while he spoke he was patting his own chest in a manner that may have expressed a sense of affinity, as if regarding the royal paragon as an expansive version of himself.

Lucy made no comment. She frowned at their shadows. His dwarfed hers, and the disparity galled her. She was conscious of how much he towered over her, how big-shouldered he was, how he seemed to bask in his manly stature. She recalled Aesop's tale about the conceited stag admiring its reflection in a forest pool in the moments before its magnificent antlers brought it to grief.

'Have you ventured into this parkland before, Miss Malpass?'

'Only once. Other things have been absorbing my attention.'

'But you do enjoy walking in these open spaces?'

'I like it better than cavorting on the carpet.'

'Such derision, coming from one who dances so gracefully!'

'Oh, it's a frivolous pastime, dancing – don't you think?'

'No, I can't agree. Dancing is an art. Patterned movement, performed by the body and shaped by the rhythms of music.'

'You might define military parade-ground drill in those same terms, but nobody would claim it deserves the status of an art form.'

Kendrick shook his head emphatically. 'Marching to a drumbeat is by no means equivalent to the complex figures of a quadrille. Dancing, at its best, is creative, surely. Elegant. It's like sculpture in motion, isn't it? Ought to belong among the fine arts.' He gestured towards the Parnassian frieze on the monument in front of them, depicting scores of notable exemplars from the fields of painting, poetry, music, sculpture and architecture. 'Dancing is quite distinct from mechanical routines such as regimental drill. And superior to merely useful handicrafts such as pottery or furniture or needlework.'

Lucy stood stock-still, a furious flush in her cheeks.

'I take strong exception to that slighting comparison,' she said, her voice rising. 'It disparages the creative skills that I cherish most. What you say, Captain, reflects masculine prejudice and ignorance. Men typically can't recognise artwork unless it's made from solid durable materials on a large scale – bronze and stone sculptures, big buildings, grandiose pictures in ostentatious frames. Women know that a needle can be employed as artfully as a paintbrush.'

Kendrick began to apologise but she swept his words aside and continued in a tone of angry vehemence. 'Our domestic crafts have every right to be recognised as art. Every right! Women understand the subtlety of small-scale decorative work. Work that doesn't strut and swagger. We love embroidery because it requires delicate handling of soft pliable fabrics. Their surfaces are subject to abrasion. Their colours can fade. Diminutive pieces of cloth may be lost or damaged. In our kind of art there's no illusion of permanence.'

'I'm sorry to have caused offence, Miss Malpass. My remarks were ill-considered. I hadn't understood the ardour of your feelings about embroidery...'

Flapping her hand dismissively, Lucy cut him short. During their return walk through the Gardens she smouldered in near silence, leaving conversational niceties to her aunt, and glowered at a boy who was bowling his hoop across their path towards a pair of doddery ducks.

'Why must you treat Kendrick so disdainfully?' Mrs Brodie asked her after the soldiers had taken their leave. 'As far as I could see, he behaved as a perfect gentleman should, and yet you seem determined to be disagreeable. I had a very pleasant conversation with his friend Barton, a well-mannered fellow, but we were both embarrassed by your obvious rudeness towards Kendrick. I won't be surprised if he makes no further contact with you.'

The following day, while her aunt was taking a postprandial nap, Lucy received another calling card from Captain Julius

Kendrick, with a message on the back of it: Miss Malpass: With deep respect, hoping to renew our conversation, J.K.

'He is waiting below?' she asked the maid, who nodded.

Pique warded off allure. 'Tell him I am not at home.'

'Beg pardon, but he knows you're in, Ma'am. He asked me directly and I said you were here.'

'Nevertheless, I am not at home to him. Please tell him so, Perkins.'

The sharp snub was sufficient. Weeks passed, then months, and he did not call again.

EIGHT

*A*S THE SEVERITY OF HER AUNT'S INJURIES BECAME clear, what made the vile assault especially distressing was that it had happened while Lucy was many miles away, enjoying the genial hospitality of the Morrises.

Two years after her arrival in London, she had been invited by May to spend a few days at the family's country home, Kelmscott House – not her first visit there, but one that marked a particular occasion.

'We have a little ritual to celebrate together on Sunday, you and I,' said May. 'A pair of dauntless damsels attaining together the perilous age of twenty-one. I've told my parents that a cheerful feast will be a suitable tribute.'

So here she was. Glancing around the large oak dining table at the assembled company – not only family members but a handful of boon companions as well – Lucy smiled to herself at the thought of their host's boyish delight in Arthurian legends. Despite its plain oblong shape, this board at which they sat so convivially must surely hold in Morris's eyes something of the mythic quality of a courtly Round Table. Gathered here were assorted peers from his arts and crafts coterie. His old friend Edward Burne-Jones sat near him, stroking a large droopy moustache and sketching something casually in a notebook while nodding agreement with anything Morris said. Next to Burne-Jones and opposite Lucy was Morris's business partner Ford Madox Brown, who had designed, she knew, some of the furniture in this house, including a washstand and dressing table that adorned the guest bedroom she was using. Now past 60, with only a few auburn streaks left in the whitening hair around his head and in his long squared-off beard, Brown looked handsome still. He was talking quietly with Philip Webb, another of Morris's partners in The Firm, as they liked to call it, and Lucy overheard Webb's comments on one of Brown's paintings. Apparently there were two versions of it, identical in composition but not in scale or medium: a small watercolour piece on paper, 'a mite too subdued' for Webb's taste, and a large canvas in oils, which he praised as 'radiant,' particularly in its play of light against dark around the glowing central garment. As the two men spoke of its depicted details, she realised that the painting's subject must be the biblical episode in which Joseph's perfidious brothers show their father Jacob the blood-stained 'coat of many colours.'

Lucy leant forward to interject. 'Might I see these paintings somewhere?' she asked eagerly.

Brown shook his head. 'Fraid not. Privately owned.'

She made a little moue of disappointment. 'Then I'll just have to content myself with imagining that brilliantly colourful coat,' she said, turning back to her food while taking sidelong note of her other dinner companions.

Morris's wife Jane, his Guinevere, sat on his left, unsmiling and wan. Conspicuously absent was Dante Rossetti, the former Lancelot, dead a year ago. Jane had been Rossetti's model, his muse, and doubtless more than that; Lucy knew the rumours, and was familiar with several of the paintings in which those unmistakable features – the ripply hair, heavy brows, pomegranate lips, prominent chin and long arching neck – were infused with a revealing ardour.

Sitting between Mrs Morris and Lucy, May seemed in profile to resemble her mother more closely than ever: that same posture, that same elongated physiognomy. As if aware of being observed, she looked around towards Lucy, placed a friendly hand on her forearm, and said with a smile, 'I've been thinking about the unusual piece of whitework embroidery you presented to me this morning – where to put it so that I can see it often. On my dressing table, I think, back in Hammersmith. It will contrast starkly with the dark wood.'

'I thought you might think it too plain, even insipid. The Mountmellick technique isn't to everyone's taste. To be frank, if I saw much of it I'd soon be reaching for the brightest coloured threads I could find. But as a birthday gift I hoped it would appeal to you, at least for its curious novelty.'

'Oh, it does. I haven't seen anything quite like it before. So fine-textured, isn't it? And the knotted, padded stitching casts faint shadows on the snowy surface – a pleasantly nuanced effect. Where did you find it?'

'A young woman who recently joined our art-needlework classes brought Mountmellick samples with her from the Irish county where her family lives. She was happy to sell me this little piece.'

'I'll study the stitching carefully, Lucy. You can be sure of that. Perhaps there are methods adaptable to our own work.'

'Meanwhile I'll be trying to learn what I can from the delicate watercolour painting you've given me. Your new honeysuckle pattern.'

'I'm pleased with it, I must confess. I've designed it with wallpaper particularly in mind.'

'It will lend itself perfectly to that. And to embroidery as well, no doubt. Your intertwining of flowers with leaves, and the way you've combined those subtle tints – the light background, the sinuous stems, and the balance of pale and dark green leaves behind the tubular flowers – I'm just itching to stitch them! So much more exacting and rewarding than some of the designs we're obliged to work with in our needlework classes.'

'The School isn't providing what you want?'

'Oh I don't mean to grumble. I can't expect it to be always exhilarating, and it does give me a certain amount of guided freedom. Freedom to experiment creatively. To set myself little challenges.'

May began to respond, but her father cut into their conversation with an anecdote that meandered around some little problem with the vats for dyeing yarns at his Merton Abbey works. Lucy's attention drifted; she found herself mulling over the mixed emotions that May's question had stirred in her. The work she had to undertake at the Art Needlework School was often on the verge of dullness, conducting her through many simple routines that gave her little satisfaction. Yet when plying a needle she soon became fully absorbed in the details of her task, visualising embellishments, imagining alternative colours and textures. Immersed in the practical challenges and aesthetic pleasures of embroidery, she would forget for a while the vacancies in her life, the losses, the bereavements. Vague images of her mother, the much more precisely imprinted memory of her father, and the accompanying swirl of feelings, would all recede while her fingers were busy with the demands of artistry. This handiwork afforded her a temporary respite, too, from the thoughts about Julius Kendrick that were never far away, pressing into her.

Emerging from her daydream, she became aware again of William Morris's stentorian voice, still holding forth on the subject of his beloved Merton Abbey works.

'But it's not only the quality of the things we're producing that gives me cause for pride,' he was saying. 'There's also our esprit de corps. All the Merton workers seem to enjoy collaborating in a comradely way – the young women at their carpet-weaving frames in the largest workshed, fabric printers on the floor above them, the group in the stained-glass studio, the apron-clad men spreading out those gorgeously dyed cloths on the sunlit grass. A little arts and crafts community, perfectly idyllic and full of high spirits – except, of course, when it rains for days on end!'

Turning to his younger daughter, 'May, my dear,' he said, 'you must bring our friend with you out to Merton some day soon. Railway connections make the journey quite simple, Miss Malpass, and I'm sure you'll fall in love with the place the moment you arrive and start looking through our cluster of quaint buildings, watching all the skilled work going on inside them. And outdoors it's a veritable wonderland: the clear waters of the River Wandle, tranquil acres of meadow and garden and orchard, with the violets and primroses in bloom…'

'It all sounds blissful,' said Lucy. 'I'd like very much to see it before long.'

'Meanwhile,' said Morris, rising from the table and patting his belly affectionately, 'now that everyone appears to be replete, I declare an end to our meal – and there's something I want to show to the young birthday ladies.'

He beckoned Lucy and May to follow him through to the panelled drawing room, where on a small side table a book of folio size lay open at its title page. It was a publication of the Society of Antiquaries, volume 6 of the *Vetusta Monumenta*, containing Charles Stothard's facsimile pictures of the Bayeux Tapestry in a set of painstakingly engraved colour-plate reproductions. Morris turned the pages slowly, enthusing over various details.

'I saw the original thing,' he said, 'a quarter of a century ago, in Normandy, when I was on vacation from Oxford with Burne-Jones and another fellow-student. Ironical and annoying that it's held in a French museum, because this so-called tapestry was almost certainly created in England. "Tapestry" is actually a misnomer, you know. It hasn't been woven on a loom. It's embroidered. Keep that in mind as you inspect these beautiful reproductions. Imagine the laborious stitching! The whole sequence consists of fifty scenes – with Latin captions, as you see here, and little additional vignettes like this along the margin. Seventy-five yards in all, hand-sewn on linen with coloured woollen yarns. Remarkably vivid, isn't it?'

He stood back, letting the women pore over the colour plates, which were more elaborately detailed than Lucy had expected, showing not just the battle scenes crowded with foot soldiers, archers and mounted horsemen but also a number of other figures, human and animal, in the borders as well as in the main panels. She stared at the pictures of naked men, with that thing between their legs, sometimes like a little snake and some-times like a big dagger. Thinking of an unclothed male body gave her a tingling sensation in the pit of her stomach. Was this, she wondered, what people meant by the term *frisson*?

'I have an idea,' Lucy told May as they came to the end of the volume and William left to rejoin his other guests. 'A little plan for reclaiming something that belongs to our culture. It seems wrong that such an important work of art, originally produced by embroiderers in this country, can only be viewed in a foreign place. What if I might persuade a group of skilled needlecraft workers here in England to produce a copy of the whole work, using these meticulously engraved colour plates as their pattern?'

'Bold scheme, Lucy! But who would take on the demands of such a project? I doubt that the patrons of your Royal School would see this as a justifiable use of its resources. Too costly.'

'Not if it could be done as a purely voluntary undertaking? By the Leek School of Embroidery, under Mrs Wardle's direction?'

'Ah! Do you really think she might be willing to manage it?'

'I'll write to her as cajolingly as I can. She's been searching, I know, for a really big challenge – something that would encourage her members to reach up together towards the highest standards of their craft.'

'I suppose Mrs Wardle fostered your passion for needlework as an art. My father said she told him you had a precocious talent.'

'Oh I learnt some useful skills from her, yes, and from other women in Leek too. But from an earlier age I was already in love with fabrics and stitches. In fact I can tell you when and how the romance began.'

As the two women sat together in the drawing room, at a comfortable distance from the drone of men's voices elsewhere in the house, Lucy reminisced dreamily about the momentous day of the picnic at Ffiney Mede just after her twelfth birthday. She could draw up every detail of it from the deep well of memory, could feel again the afternoon's warmth on her skin after the meal, could see herself lying back on a rug with hands clasped beneath her head, bonnet tipped forward to shield her face from the sun.

'Contentment seemed to fill me,' she told May, 'and brighten everything around me.' Her cheerful mood had been ephemeral; an hour later it would turn mottled and muddled. But she said nothing of that now. Instead she recounted what her factory-owner father had explained that day about the difficult business of manufacturing silk, which she had previously understood only in the simplest terms – raw silk was imported, made somehow into coloured thread and then woven on machines. As she rested with him on the meadow grass, he gave her an insight into the complexity of the whole process: how vital it had become to keep up with new techniques of dyeing and weaving, how intensely competitive it was as costs kept rising while producers undercut each other's prices, how hard he found it to hire and train reliable workers for every specialised job – the twisters, dressers, throwsters and the rest.

'As he spoke,' she told May, 'my imagination seemed to inhabit a sunny silken world. I remember lying there with my eyes closed and picturing the qualities of silk, its smoothness and its shimmer and its rustle, its magical trick of making fabric flow like a liquid, its ability to invest its many colours with an intensity that was almost luminous.'

'So that was the beginning of your love affair with silken thread?'

'With thread in all its varieties, spun from so many different fibres to be sewn and woven into so many different textile materials. Silk for me is certainly the queen of fabrics but of course I admire cotton too, and linen, and wool, each in its own way marvellous to look at and to handle.'

As May listened intently, Lucy went on to describe another revelation that came to her that afternoon on Ffiney Mede. She had opened her eyes at the sound of bickering birds, and a couple of chaffinches hopped close to her, fat fellows with russet-pink breasts and grey heads framing their chestnut cheeks, both birds in pursuit of the same insects. Their little squabble made her laugh. Sitting up and looking around, she noticed that the meadow was splashed with floral colour. Nearest to her were oxeye daisies with golden yolk-like centres. 'They're like fried eggs with serrated edges,' she told her father. He smiled as he drank more barley wine, and pointed to a bright pink knapweed flower just behind her: it had a red admiral butterfly perching on it in search of nectar.

Suddenly, for the first time in her twelve-year-old life, she had felt entranced by the great mystery of colour. What is it, she pondered, that makes one thing strike the eye as red and another as green? Why do some tints go together harmoniously while others clash? Why does a dress of blue and gold have a sumptuous appearance while a brown one looks drab, frumpish? Black and white: are they actually colours, or devoid of colour?

As the whole scene and its associated feelings came back to her, renewing a sense of wonder, she said to May, 'A colourless world, completely blank, would drive me insane.'

Returning blithely to the De Vere Gardens flat that evening after dark, her head still full of lofty thoughts about ambitious design projects and communities of artists, Lucy was met at the outer door by their maidservant, whose red eyes and handwringing alarmed her immediately.

'Whatever's wrong, Perkins?'

'Oh it's Mrs Brodie, Ma'am. Someone's gone and attacked her on the steps outside, late this afternoon, and her head's been hurt bad. A nasty gash on her temple and bruising around one eye, and she don't seem able to talk any sense. I called for Dr Bain, and he's come quick, left here only half an hour ago. Gave her something to calm her, he did, and says someone should sit with her during the night. Watch over her, is how he put it. She could take a sudden turn for the worse, he says. Oh, what a thing to happen in a respectable neighbourhood like this!'

'It's dreadful. But why... Was it robbery?'

'Must've been, yes, because her silk reticule was gone when we found her.'

'A common footpad, then – here, in broad daylight! Snatching a lady's reticule is brazen enough, but why strike her violently?'

'Well, it may be he didn't, you see. The way the doctor looks at it, Mrs Brodie probably struggles with this man, so then he pushes her aside, or anyhow she just falls heavily, and bang! – hits her head on the railing.'

Hurrying up the staircase, Lucy went straight to her aunt's bedside. The mouth was open, the breaths shallow and rasping. Puffy eyes stared blankly from the bandaged face. No sign of recognition. No answer when Lucy spoke to her. No response to a gentle pressure on her fingers. This was a mere husk of the person with whom she had been living.

NINE

EMERGING UNSTEADILY FROM HER MENTAL FOG AFTER A couple of days, Barbara Brodie insisted on being up and about, though her faculties were still obviously impaired and her behaviour soon proved erratic. One morning a shriek from Perkins brought Lucy running into an upstairs bedroom: her aunt was attempting to climb out of the window. When restrained, she pulled free and began to dash her forehead against the marble mantelpiece, grunting and bleating.

Worried that her aunt, if left unattended, might put herself in further danger at home or wander off down the street and forget her whereabouts, Lucy sent word to the Art Needlework School, asking to be excused from attendance for the next month because she must 'care for a family member who had fallen ill.' *Fallen ill*: the odd phrase resounded in Lucy's head as she came to see how painfully difficult it was to take care of someone who went on falling, falling, into further strangeness. There were several alarming episodes. Barbara Brodie strewed pieces of clothing around the flat. Then, seizing a pair of scissors, she hacked at her own hair until the scalp looked like a frowsy grey stubble field. Within a week she had become quite unmanageable, refusing food and neglecting all habits of cleanliness.

'I'm sorry to confirm,' said Dr Bain, 'that your aunt is now quite out of her mind, and there seems little prospect of recovery.'

As she dabbed at tears, Lucy tried to compose herself. 'What should I do, then?'

Titus Bain leant forward, thin fingers gripping the silver knob on his walking cane, tongue-tip moistening his ginger moustache. 'Impossible for her to be safely supervised here,' he said. 'Mrs Brodie's condition has become very serious. She'll need close professional attention throughout the day. Indefinitely, I'm afraid. Too much to expect of you or your maidservant.'

'So then, we must commit her to a madhouse, d'you mean?'

'That, I believe, is the only responsible course of action, Miss Malpass. The idea shocks you, I can see. But she deserves the safety of a place where trained staff can look after her with all the resources of medical science.'

'Do you know of such a place? One you can recommend whole-heartedly?'

Dr Bain nodded. Pulling out a large blue silk handkerchief, he polished his spectacles slowly as he began to answer her.

'I do: it's called Ticehurst House. High standards, excellent reputation. I've been there a couple of times to see patients and professional colleagues, and I don't hesitate to say that it offers better accommodation, services and medical skill than any other private asylum in the country. Well appointed, well staffed.'

'I know nothing about it. Where is this place?'

'East Sussex. Not far beyond Tunbridge Wells. You'd be able to pay frequent visits quite easily.'

Lucy pressed her fingers to her brow. 'Good quality accommodation, you say. All the same, I suppose it must be a thoroughly wretched place for the inmates. The thought of my poor dear aunt being treated like a prisoner, and mixing with madmen whose behaviour might distress her…'

'No no, Ticehurst isn't like that at all, Miss Malpass. It's a private establishment, you see, a licensed house, so it isn't swarming with all sorts of lunatics, as the county asylums tend to be. The average annual fee at Ticehurst is relatively high, near to 500 pounds I believe, which means she'll be comfortable there among people of her own class. Its residents include a good number of independent gentlewomen and gentlemen with a secure income. There are also merchants, financiers, clergymen, barristers and the like, from all parts of the British Isles.'

'The quarters are not oppressively cramped, then?'

'By no means. Spacious rooms, and fewer than four score of patients. To cater for their needs, Ticehurst employs about twice that number of servants and attendants. Half a dozen lady companions, as well, are on hand to assist female patients with music, drawing, sewing, pastimes of that kind.'

'But would she be cooped up in her room most of the time?'

'Far from it. The proprietors, the Newingtons, estimable family, take an enlightened view of treatment. They encourage walks around the extensive grounds and ornamental gardens, and provide other outdoor activities to exercise the body and stimulate the mind. Or quieten the spirit, if need be. Those too weak to walk far are taken for carriage rides. Indoors, I've been told, there are musical concerts from time to time, and patients can also play chess, cribbage, whist and other soothing games.'

'But violence must sometimes erupt?'

'Oh, it's not a significant problem, I assure you. Whatever delusions and diseases the patients may suffer, they generally pose no personal threat to one another. For those who may need occasionally to be calmed, temporary seclusion is available at some distance from other patients.'

The process of admitting Mrs Brodie to Ticehurst, though probably bewildering to her and certainly troubling to her niece, was completed without difficulty or protest. In Lucy's heart, relief mingled with self-reproach. While solaced by the knowledge that Aunt Barbara's treatment would now be in the hands of well-qualified professional people, she could not avoid a guilty sense of abandoning this person who had so conscientiously looked after her. She seethed with anger, too, at the thought that the life of such a kindly and intelligent woman could be damaged so suddenly, so brutally, by the wanton act of a common felon.

Although these different strands of feeling remained knotted tight, Lucy's first impressions of Ticehurst House had brought reassurance. The handsome buildings, neatly appointed, were set within serene environs – in all, an orderly place but not subject to obtrusive control. Greeting them cordially on their arrival, Dr Hayes Newington spoke without condescension, handled the admission formalities without fuss, and seemed to be a compassionate man. The nurse who then conducted them to Mrs Brodie's new quarters and explained the practical arrangements had a tactful manner that implied respect for the patient's dignity. Here, Lucy could imagine, her aunt would find balm for her injured spirit.

Returning now a fortnight later to visit her, Lucy spent most of the journey from London – by rail to Tunbridge Wells, then by carriage on the turnpike road to Ticehurst – absorbed in a cloud of anxious musings. If, as Dr Titus Bain predicted, her aunt was likely to require medical support in this institution for the rest of her days, what might this mean for Lucy's own future? Should she stay on in London indefinitely, alone? Doing what? Could the continuing expense of Ticehurst fees be fully met from Mrs Brodie's financial resources, assuming that Lucy was permitted to draw on these? Or might they need eventually to be supplemented from the much less substantial funds that Lucy had inherited from her father's debt-laden estate? As the carriage took her through the gates of Ticehurst and up its long winding driveway, she resolved to discuss such matters with a lawyer once she was back in London.

Lucy had sent a letter ahead to notify Ticehurst's proprietor of her intended arrival time. Now, confirming at the reception office that Mrs Brodie was waiting in her room, she proceeded there. Her aunt sat hunched in an armchair, head bent forward and eyes lowered. She made no response to her visitor's greeting. The attendant nurse whispered to Lucy, 'We managed to calm her down this morning with hydrotherapy. She'll probably remain quite docile for the next few hours.'

'I'd like to take her outside for a walk in the grounds,' said Lucy. 'The afternoon is agreeably mild.'

'Strolling along the garden paths will suit her condition well, Miss Malpass. Fresh air can be a healthy tonic. Shall I accompany you?'

'No need, thank you. We won't go far. I can call for assistance if anything untoward happens.'

Despite her stooping posture, Mrs Brodie had not suffered any apparent physical enfeeblement, and the walking seemed to reinvigorate her. From the southern entrance of the main building they made their way to a formal garden terrace enclosed on three sides by a low rock wall inset with small jardinières. Steps led down from the terrace to a gravel path, and then to a wide lawn that gave them panoramic views of the Rother valley.

At the far end of the lawn they found a rock arch, and beyond the arch a fernery encircled by a bank of earth. Lifting his hat with a flourish, a thin neatly dressed man rose from a garden seat in front of them as they entered the fernery.

'Good afternoon, ladies. Ah, Mrs Brodie, how are you?' She gave no answer. He turned to Lucy. 'And you, madam, are a family visitor, I presume? Dr Thomas Bracken at your service.'

Lucy introduced herself, and there was a brief exchange of pleasantries about weather and landscape. Then Bracken's tone abruptly changed. Frowning, he told Lucy with earnest concern, 'I'm considering a change of treatment for Mrs Brodie.'

'Oh?'

'Yes. A new regimen altogether. Enormous doses of brandy, morning, noon and night!' He let out a trill of high-pitched laughter, accompanied by a performance of rapid little shrugs, as if to signal that his shoulders were rippling with mirthfulness.

Then, reverting just as suddenly to a demeanour of solemn gravity, he leant towards Lucy and said in a confidential manner, 'The attendants can't be trusted with the food and drink, you know. I have to be vigilant.'

Startled, she stared at him. 'Vigilant about food and drink? What do you mean, Dr Bracken?'

'And poisoning isn't the only hazard. There's also the spiteful way they assault some of the patients. But I know how to deal with that. Forestall them by striking first, before they can lift a hand!' Again he gave his peculiar warbling laugh, with the same supplementary series of shoulder-jerks. Just at that moment a pair of male attendants came hurrying up.

'Ah! There you are, Mr Bracken. Gave us the slip again. Come along now.' One on either side of him, holding his forearms gently but firmly, they conducted him towards the asylum building.

Lucy looked at her aunt with raised eyebrows, but Mrs Brodie, lost in lethargy, gave no sign of having understood anything Bracken had said, and was unresponsive to Lucy's attempts to converse as they walked slowly back towards her room.

Later that afternoon as Lucy was about to get into her carriage for the journey back to Tunbridge Wells, the Ticehurst proprietor, Hayes Newington, approached her. 'May I detain you for a moment, Miss Malpass?' he asked, going on to say that he had just heard about the 'little incident with our Mr Bracken,' and wished to apologise. 'We try to keep a close watch on him, but he can be quite sly, and slippery as an eel. Never dangerous to anyone, despite his frequently odd behaviour, though from time to time he does make some of the other patients feel somewhat agitated.'

'I suppose he's never been a physician at all?'

'Was once, actually, but an unfortunate episode a few years ago led to his committal to Ticehurst. He'd become convinced that he was the subject of a conspiracy instigated by rival doctors and supported by the police, the post office, the local curate, even his family. Felt utterly alone, poor fellow, and still feels it here. Doesn't trust anybody. Sad business.'

'Sad indeed. A case of "Physician, heal thyself," I suppose.'

'And several others at Ticehurst are similarly isolated, cut off from companionship by their imaginings. You see it in your aunt. A disturbed mind can be the most solitary of afflictions, Miss Malpass. We do all we can to remedy that problem by creating, as far as possible, a family attitude here.' He feels their distress deeply, Lucy thought, and I'm sure he does his best to manage it with discretion. She thanked Newington for the efforts that he and his staff were making to care for her aunt and others in their charge. 'Many of your patients,' she said, 'would find more benefit, I well believe, in the tranquil home-like atmosphere you create than any medicinal treatments could provide.'

'We're convinced of that, certainly. Of course we do make judicious use of medicines, especially purgatives – castor oil, rhubarb pills, senna draughts. And the sedative effect of cold mustard baths has proved salutary for a few patients. But above all, it's the sense of belonging to something like a family group that can do most to ease their maladies. However, I mustn't keep you talking, Miss Malpass. Your carriage awaits you, and the shadows are lengthening.'

Insanity? What is it? The question tumbled around in her mind as horse and then steam took her towards London. During her visit she had observed a few patients who were plainly disturbed and others who seemed completely normal. Granted, these were the merest glimpses; had she been there the previous day, or the next, she might well have witnessed quite different behaviour from these same people. Still, the line that separated the mad from the unmad was mysteriously blurred. She thought of May Morris's elder sister Jenny, whose 'nervous condition,' as the family called it, expressed itself in fits and erratic tempers. Were these different from symptoms of insanity? Lucy had even heard some people speak of William Morris himself as 'a half-lunatic genius.' Perhaps every person of artistic temperament was partly mad. Was she herself, with what her aunt had once described as a fierce and fiery spirit, always entirely rational and lucid?

TEN

---

*I*T WAS A FURTHER YEAR AND A HALF BEFORE ANYTHING OUT of the ordinary happened to Lucy. Months and seasons had passed in an uneventful procession. She paid dutifully regular visits to Ticehurst, finding each time that her aunt's condition persisted without significant change. She continued with her needlework classes, as the activity was generally agreeable enough and there seemed to be no better way of occupying herself for the time being. She stayed on in the comfortable De Vere Gardens flat with Perkins as her servant, having ascertained that there were no legal or financial problems about modifying the lease arrangement, and that her situation was secure for the foreseeable future. She remained close to May Morris, enjoying not only frequent contact with the Hammersmith circle but also a number of excursions to Kelmscott House and the Merton Abbey Works. Her life, she reflected with a wistful sigh, had settled into a calm routine that was moderately pleasant for the most part, sometimes engrossing, but devoid of any exhilarating surprise.

Then, on a bitterly cold day in mid-November 1883, came an unpredictable encounter that overturned her usual composure.

She had arranged to rendezvous with May in the South Kensington Museum of Arts, as they usually did on Wednesday afternoons after May finished for the day at the School of Design. Always arriving ahead of the appointed time, Lucy would drift from gallery to gallery, from one cabinet to another, relishing the variety of exhibits, ruminating on the aesthetic choices made by their makers. She knew that this Museum, now occupying a large space bordered by Exhibition Road and Cromwell Road, had grown from collections put together to support teaching in the School of Design, which was housed on the same site. In addition to the many thousands of donated and purchased items, the collections were augmented by some of the finest British, European and oriental pieces of medieval and modern workmanship on loan from private owners.

The two women always met in the east arcade of the North Court, where a large assortment of woven fabrics was on permanent display, including rare samples of medieval embroidery. At this moment Lucy was leaning over a glass case, absorbed in her scrutiny of one of the Museum's most precious textile acquisitions, a fragment of the medieval Cloth of St Gereon. Woven in faded dark green and rust-brown wool, this small portion of the border showed a staring lion head surrounded by symmetrical coiling stalks. The German mural tapestry from which the piece had been cut, a small caption declared, was 'possibly the oldest surviving work of its kind produced anywhere in Europe.' A finely drawn picture beside the caption showed the full design: it depicted a recurrent pattern of roundels enclosing a decorative motif of a griffin overpowering a bull. The semi-human face of the bull looked out disconsolately towards the viewer.

There were heavy footsteps behind her, and then someone spoke her name. Though she had not heard the vibrancy of this voice for a long while, she knew at once that it belonged to Captain Julius Kendrick.

Even taller and more imposing than she remembered, he stood there with his friend Barton beside him, both bending forward in bows of formal greeting, both resplendent in their scarlet tunics. Her mouth opened, closed and opened again while she was searching for words. They came out coldly.

'An unlikely place for you to be loitering, Captain. Men in uniform seem incongruous here.'

'Not so. We've been to this part of the Museum several times.'

As she looked at him sceptically, he added, 'So much beautiful work to learn from.'

'Oh, it's beautiful work now, is it? I haven't forgotten how you spoke of embroidery in a dismissive way, as if it were a trivial feminine "accomplishment" and not, in its finest expression, an art form worthy of respect.'

'I didn't mean to give offence on that occasion, Miss Malpass. I know I spoke clumsily, though to be frank I must say you seemed eager to seize on perceived slights. But do forgive me, if you can, for my boorish remarks. I admit I'd known almost nothing about embroidery. I used to associate it with a dreary cousin of mine who spent hours on end frowning over a basket of hand-worked cambric stuff for her trousseau, stitching away listlessly. No doubt you were justified in rebuking me for my ignorance, which I've tried to rectify since then by coming here when I have a leisure hour or two. Barton is kind enough to accompany me so that I don't look singularly out of place. We've been studying the textile displays with close attention.'

'So by now, I suppose, you must be quite the connoisseur.'

'Ah, you're mocking me, and perhaps it's deserved. At any rate, I should confess to another motive for visiting this place from time to time. I've been hoping that I might find you here one day.'

Declining to respond, she forced herself to hold Kendrick's level gaze. Barton tactfully moved away to inspect some glass showcases in another part of the arcade.

Kendrick broke the awkward silence with a plea. 'Can we put our disagreements behind us?'

She answered with a confused gesture, half shrugging, half smiling. 'Well, Captain...' she began uncertainly – and then broke off as May entered the room and came towards them. Briefly introducing her friend, Lucy linked arms with her, told Kendrick that they had a train to catch, and walked off in a brusque leave-taking. May's later questions were brushed aside.

The following Wednesday she came early to the same nook of the Museum, and was unsurprised to find him already there again, but alone. This time her frame of mind was receptive. Before long they were sitting together on an ornate wooden bench against the arcade wall, talking without effort or constraint. In the course of nearly an hour their conversation turned this way and that, through all manner of topics. Encouraged by his tactful questioning, she talked freely about what had befallen her aunt, and the practical consequences of that calamity; about how perturbed she herself felt during her visits to Ticehurst, not least because the borderline between madness and emotional inten-sity seemed to her so indistinct; about her childhood in Leek, disrupted by the accidental death of her father; about finding her vocation through the Leek Embroidery Society with Mrs Wardle's encouragement; about how she had been persuaded to make the move to London, where the talented and generous Morris family had befriended her; and about her ambivalence towards classes at the Needlework School.

He spoke with reciprocal candour about army life, its bursts of excitement and long stretches of utter tedium; about mundane aspects of life in India, where his regiment had spent most of the last year and where he would be returning by the end of the month, when his period of leave expired; about his parents, his sisters, and the cherished old family property near Winchester; and about Gerard Barton, his foster-brother and closest comrade in arms.

They were now at ease with each other. Her doubts about this man evaporated; disputes were quickly forgotten. By the time May arrived, Lucy was afloat on a pond of elation, enfolded in a sense of being somehow simultaneously tranquil and exuberant. She saw that May registered at once the undisguised change in her attitude. When the two women left the Museum together and made their way along the street Lucy relinquished all defensiveness, disclosing that Kendrick had begun to stir her affections deeply.

'And unreservedly?' May's astute question brought Lucy to a halt.

'I don't know him well enough to say that. Still a few reservations, probably. Just intuitive. I'm not sure I could put them into words at the moment.'

A letter came from him a couple of days later, telling her that the date of his departure for India had been brought forward by nearly a week. Much needed to be done before the regiment would be ready to embark; he was obliged to busy himself urgently with all sorts of intensive preparations, such as drawing up a schedule of travel instructions for the rank and file, supervising certain equipment inventories, and so forth. He hoped that, without inconvenience to her, he might pay her a visit at the De Vere Gardens flat this next Sunday afternoon, which would be his only opportunity to see her.

❖

From the moment of his arrival on Sunday, Lucy felt perversely ill-humoured and could find nothing welcoming to say. Whether to guard against showing emotion at the imminent loss of him, or for some more obscure reason, she hardened her voice and implicitly repudiated their previous conversational rapport.

When he asked if he might address her by her first name, she demurred. 'A little premature, I rather think.' She didn't understand what made her say that. When he complimented her on the delicate mulberry-coloured tea gown, so carefully chosen, she tried to respond with a self-deprecating phrase but knew it sounded like a snub. When he said her healthy complexion suggested that she must have been undertaking salubrious exercise in the Kensington Gardens, she replied haughtily that his flattery was unconvincing, and she had been much too busy for idle sauntering.

He looked bemused by her contrary tone, but made another attempt. 'I'm not taken in, Miss Malpass, by your pretence of ignoring how very elegant you look. You must be aware by now that, in my eyes, you possess a quite exceptional charm.'

Stifling an involuntary smile of gratification, she lifted an eyebrow. 'How laboriously gallant of you to say so, Captain.'

'Please don't treat my words as if they were part of a little game of chivalry. I'm completely sincere, I assure you. I'm trying to express what I feel. If my declaration seems untimely, or somehow too bold, I hope you'll see that I'm speaking now in these direct terms because I must leave England very soon and be absent for some while. I don't want to do go without persuading you, if I can, to join me in a pledge…'

'Pledge?'

'Committing ourselves to a shared future. Vowing to belong to each other…'

She bristled. 'Belong? Belong! I don't want to belong to anybody, ever! I'm not a commodity to be possessed.'

He looked stricken, but then raised his chin and squared his shoulders. 'You're quarrelling with a mere word. Can't you acknowledge what it's obvious I mean to convey? I'm a plain soldier, not a poet with a gift of the gab, but my feelings for you are no less genuine for that. And I'm sure you feel the same way about me. Very sure. Our long recent conversation at the Museum – it was perfectly harmonious, wasn't it? It confirmed my belief that we are twin spirits, despite our different circumstances. That's all I meant by saying we belong to each other. I fervently hope you'll agree that as soon as I return from India we...'

She could not stop herself from interrupting hastily to fend away his declaration before it became a more explicit proposal.

'There's something presumptuous behind your words,' she said in a flare of ill temper. 'You strike me as cocksure but trying not to show it.'

Exasperated, he gave a mirthless laugh. 'That's nonsense. I think you know you're being wilfully unjust. You seem to be gripped by some kind of panic, as if the thought of getting closer to each other makes you afraid.'

His words had the sting of truth, and to her dismay she felt tears welling up. She turned her head away.

'I'm...I'm...' She stopped, not knowing what she was.

'I see I've upset you somehow, Miss Malpass. If I try to say more I'll probably make matters worse. It's time now for me to go, regretfully. But I do intend to write to you while I'm overseas, if I may?'

She nodded in silence, and could not look at him as he left the room.

It would be a long time before she saw him again in person; but that night, as she lay sleepless and febrile, he loomed up in her mind's eye like a powerful animal, thick-shouldered, heavily muscled. His wiry beard and the dark hair on the back of his large hands exuded virility. This image brought with it something from the past: the time when, as a girl, she had watched in fascination a massive bull in a field near her home as, with seemingly inexhaustible fecundity, it covered cow after cow and still wanted more.

She climbed out of her bed, lit a candle, faced the cheval mirror and tilted her head slowly from one side to the other, giving herself a tentative appraisal. Drew her waist in. Slowly removed her nightdress to stand there completely naked, until confused memories of a day from the distant past crept into a corner of her mind and she began to shake with suppressed sobs.

ELEVEN

HE DID WRITE TO HER FROM INDIA, BUT EVEN IN THE early phase of his absence the letters came infrequently and failed to slake her thirst for – for…? His words on the page lacked something she wanted, but she felt unsure what it was. Self-disclosure, in part: very little of the inner man could be glimpsed behind his suave formality. And when looking outwards what did he see? If he had interesting opinions on the world around him, he kept them to himself. Only scant information about Indian life trickled into his correspondence. Lucy could glean no sense of what that vast country was really like, and what it had in common with her own, beyond the peculiar fact that the Queen of England was also somehow the Empress of India. Indians had dark skins, she knew, and produced beautiful silken fabrics, but that was almost the extent of her knowledge, and Kendrick's letters did little to make her less ignorant. Aside from passing general mentions of heat and disease and poverty, the things he wrote conveyed little impression of how local inhabitants lived. Although she hadn't expected him to provide much detail, there was hardly anything to indicate what Indian people wore, or ate, or did, or believed. Nothing, either, to explain the significance of the exotic-sounding places he mentioned, Secunderabad, Cannanore, Madras and the rest: what and where were they, and why was his regiment camped there? How did he and his fellow officers spend their time? Those 'sepoys,' native infantry under British command: were they serving alongside the white soldiers, like equals? Were the Englishmen engaged in any fighting? Did they face a greater threat from mutinous Indians than from tigers or elephants or other strange beasts? Perhaps Captain Kendrick was too preoccupied with his military duties (but what exactly were they?) to be an interesting correspondent. Or was he just not very observant?

Besides, what of his feelings towards her? Cloudy phrases made them indistinct. His letters merely declared that he 'often thought about' the few occasions spent with her, and 'dearly missed' their conversations, 'tense though these sometimes were.' However, he did raise the topic that she had forestalled when they were last together:

> I intend to pursue at a later stage my question about sharing our future, but meanwhile I'm duty-bound to stay here. While it's not unknown for womenfolk to travel out from England to wed officers and reside temporarily in India, it would be quite unfair to ask that of you. The lot of a military wife can be unpleasant, especially away from our home country. The barracks here are cramped and unsanitary, and although we have very little social contact with ordinary soldiers their proximity can sometimes be irksome. To be candid, I must say that we see too many ruffians in the ranks, men who enlisted only because they were desperate and unemployed. Besides, there is talk among the

officers about the likelihood that our regiment may be deployed even further east sooner or later. If the rumours are correct, trouble is brewing in Burma. In short, Miss Malpass, east of Suez is no place for a refined young Englishwoman. For my own part, I confess that the lure of military adventure will keep me here for some while before I can envisage returning to England. I do hope you will wait for me.

She replied to each of his letters, but never immediately or at length, and always in a tone of cool restraint. She doubted that he was aware of any whiff of arrogance in making the warrior life his explicit priority while saying he wished her to be patient. Evidently he wasn't much given to reflective inwardness, this man. Nevertheless a clear physical image of him stayed with her constantly: burly, thickset, bull-shouldered, yet moving with poise.

Moving with poise: this thought recalled her aunt's appreciative comment, after the tea dance at Mrs Watson's house, on Kendrick's deportment: 'a nimble-footed dancer,' she remarked, 'for such a tall and muscular man.' Lucy had never fully admitted to herself, let alone been able to explain to her aunt, why dancing with Kendrick on that occasion unsettled her as it did, stirring a murky emotional sediment in which hungry need was obscurely mixed with apprehension. But she sensed that these viscous and troubled feelings had a much earlier source. Her memory slid hastily away from it.

In July 1884 something unexpected brought to the surface Lucy's swelling frustration at the limits imposed on her creativity. Other half-submerged feelings rose up with it.

Under royal patronage an ambitious International Health Exhibition had opened in South Kensington, just a short walk away from Lucy's flat. On a spacious site beside Queens Gate, between the newly opened Natural History Museum and the Royal Albert Hall, the exhibition assembled offerings from many cultures. It covered everything that might conceivably promote hygiene in the populace – from sanitary appliances to health education, from various kinds of clothing and foodstuffs to an array of exemplary furniture, interior design and handicrafts. Week after week huge crowds moved gawping through the building. One moist warm evening at May's suggestion, Lucy went along to the central gallery with her to hear a spirited public lecture by William Morris on the history of textile production. In jaunty conversation afterwards as the audience dispersed, he urged them both to see 'the little display of Icelandic craftwork, modest but remarkable, put together by Sigridur Magnusson' – wife of his literary collaborator. It was in the western annexe, he told them.

So she wandered with May through the extensive display areas, examining samples of needlework from Japan, China, Switzerland, Belgium and India before finding the Icelandic exhibits in an inconspicuous corner: a small array of handmade woollen goods and embroideries. Among these items, one stood out. It was a large coverlet, which arrested her attention because its main features forcefully reminded her of the more elaborate and mysterious design she had once been shown in William Morris's own study, the watercolour that he himself had executed while in Reykjavík, copying it from an old wall hanging.

In the same mannered way, both this coverlet before her now and the design reproduced by Morris had placed strange human shapes in cryptic juxtaposition and framed them within a chain of medallions. Some of them wore masks that made her think again of dancing mummers. A particularly compelling feature, taking sudden hold of her imagination, was their hint of an underlying ferocity. These angular figures from the isolated northern world so ardently evoked by Morris, a wild, brutal, outlandish place, formed a striking contrast with many of the patterns, tame and pallid, that governed her training at the Needlework School.

Contemplating the exhibit with her friend at her side, Lucy couldn't contain her restless feelings in silence.

'I'm chafing, May!' she burst out. 'Chafing at my daily routine of work! It's come to seem so...so decorously constrained. Devoid of the passion that this bold Icelandic design embodies.'

May gave her a searching look. 'I knew you had reservations about what the School requires you to do, but I hadn't understood how much it irritates you.'

'Oh, it's not that I'm ungrateful for everything I've learnt about techniques, but I do wish our instructors would devote less attention to embellishing mundane items. I've handled too many hassock covers and glorified knick-knacks. I'm greedy for more testing opportunities. More complex patterns. More scope for the kinds of artistry encouraged in your studios at the Design School. Artistry and ingenuity. Whenever you talk of what you do there, I feel envious.'

'I'm fortunate, I know. There's such a stimulating variety of things to occupy our time.'

Lucy linked her arm through May's, and they began to move towards the exit. 'Tell me about some of the work you've been doing there lately.'

'It changes frequently. Last week we devoted most of our time to drawing parts of the human figure. Heads and shoulders, hands and forearms. It's a lovely space, the Life Room, up there on the third storey, well lit from the north in clear weather, though sooty air does dim the light coming in from outside. And since then we've been studying one of the medieval treasures in the museum next door, the Great Cope of Syon. Fourteenth century. Produced by nuns in an abbey in Middlesex. You've seen it?'

'I have. Beautiful execution, so exact. You don't find the subject matter too suffocatingly religious?'

'Oh, its piety has no appeal for me, of course – we Morrises are thoroughly pagan, as you know. But I do love the visual harmony of it all. Such a masterpiece of practical design! The ingenious way in which all those human and angelic figures are arranged – there's great power in it, don't you think? Radiating out from the centre of the semi-circular garment, so that they'd appear upright when a bishop was wearing it to celebrate mass. It balances colours and textures perfectly: the linen background worked over entirely with laid and couched work in red and green silk, and the contrasting biblical figures, done with split stitch.'

'Yes, the quality of the stitching is certainly very fine.'

'You see it, don't you, in those saintly faces, rendered with such minute precision that the play of light is quite striking. On cheekbones, chins, noses, throats. And the technique of under-side couching allows the silver and gilt threads to shimmer. Shimmer and glitter in movement.'

'You have such a memorable turn of phrase, May, when you're describing embroidery. I wish you'd pen some articles on the subject for publication.'

'As it happens, I'm planning to write a book on decorative needlework, setting out its principles. Well, "planning" is an overstatement. I'm toying with the idea of such a book, but I expect a few years will pass before I can find time to complete it. Meanwhile it seems I'll have my hands full – continuing at the Design School for the rest of this year, and after that there's likely to be a role that my father has in mind for me.'

Stopping, Lucy turned towards her friend. 'Is the role a secret?'

'It won't be mentioned publicly for some months yet, but I'm glad to tell you about it. My father has foreshadowed that he wants me to take charge of the Embroidery Department at the Merton Abbey Works.'

'Ah! And you yourself – you do want this position?'

'Oh yes. I couldn't be keener. I'm sure there's scope to expand that side of the enterprise. And now that the matter has come up, Lucy, there's something I'd like to mention. Do please consider whether employment at the Merton Abbey Works may be the most congenial way for you to spend your time in the future.'

'Working for you there! I'd love to do that!'

'But in the spirit of working *with* me, of course, not as an underling.'

They sealed their understanding with an exchange of broad sisterly smiles, and moved outside together into the thick brown air of the street, their faces dimly illuminated by the gas lamps.

During the early months of 1885 Lucy's sense that her life was undergoing an enlargement seemed to be amplified by momentous happenings in the wider world.

At the Merton Abbey Works she revelled in the challenge of devising subtle techniques for embroidering what May designed, and sometimes venturing to suggest how this or that particular pattern might be adapted to different fabrics. The daily journey from the city into the countryside always lifted her spirits, and the workplace itself held many little pleasures. All the sights and smells and sounds filled her with delight. She worked assiduously at her own tasks but when there were occasional lulls she liked to stand for a few moments in the biggest shed and watch the rows of women at their weaving frames, surrounded by an array of bobbins, shuttles and coloured worsteds; or to peep into the dyeshop, where muttering men in clogs moved from one copper beck to another; or in fine weather to step outdoors, away from the noisy Jacquard looms, gazing at the bright skeins of silk piled together on a trestle and the yards of floral chintz spread on the grass to dry.

While being part of this community of artisans was enjoyable in its own right, Lucy felt further satisfaction in seeing their activities as politically significant. Through May's tutelage she was learning to think of the Arts and Crafts movement as a socialist enterprise. By reforming the processes of manufacture, those who worked in a spirit of creative freedom at Merton Abbey and through a growing number of other such groups around the country would, she expected, eventually liberate industrial society from the ugliness that disfigured it. She found herself drawn towards the newly formed Socialist League, whose chief founder and leading figure was William Morris. He edited its monthly magazine, *The Commonweal*, which Lucy read conscientiously. Many of the articles that filled its pages came from his hand, and their rousing rhetoric stirred her imagination. It was, he thundered, a loss of pride in assiduous workmanship that had caused England's towns to become 'sordid and hideous, insults to the beauty of the earth.' Most of the common people were now enslaved by their labour. Only through rediscovering the simple yet artful pleasure of 'free and happy work' could they escape this miserable condition.

She could see that the Socialist League had not timed its emergence propitiously. A few weeks after its first meeting it was pushed to an outer margin of public attention by the sensational news that General Gordon, Governor-General of the Sudan, had been killed in the siege of Khartoum. Widely revered as a martyr courageous in upholding British ideals and defying Muslim brutality, Gordon was less admirable in the eyes of a critical minority for whom Britain's actions in the dark continent, as the adventurer Henry Morton Stanley had called it, began to seem just as rapacious as those of Belgium in annexing the Congo or Germany in seizing a slab of East Africa. At public meetings, in letters, and in the pages of *The Commonweal*, Morris and his Socialist League brethren fulminated against 'the imperialist-jingo game' and decried the Sudanese war as serving the interests of a marauding capitalist class; but it was obvious to Lucy that their protests were failing to garner general support. Other outrages crowded the newspaper headlines. Within England, Fenians had intensified their campaign of bombing railway stations and public buildings. Gladstone's Liberal government, hurt by strident disputes over Irish home rule, was defeated by a vote of no confidence. *The Pall Mall Gazette's* scandalous exposure of white slavery revealed how easily girls as young as thirteen could be procured in London for prostitution, and soon afterwards parliament passed an act that raised the age of consent to sixteen.

In such an overheated climate of disputation, citizens with a leaning towards radical left-wing ideas were more likely to be attracted to the rival Fabian Society, which – unlike the Socialist

League – pragmatically pursued the cause of parliamentary reform, doing so with unmatched brio. The League's manifesto, written by Morris and published in *The Commonweal*, was less forceful than the one produced a few months earlier for the Fabians. May read portions of this Fabian tract aloud to Lucy, not only expressing admiration of its wit but also confessing to infatuation with its author.

Lucy gaped at her. 'In love with Bernard Shaw?'

'GBS, none other. I want you to meet him and tell me what you think. His manner can be odd, but you'll soon see why I'm smitten.'

TWELVE

WAITING FOR OTHERS TO ARRIVE AS AUTUMNAL darkness thickened outside, they sat in the candlelit drawing room of Kelmscott House: two voluble men, two watchful women. In half an hour a Socialist League meeting was due to begin and they were expecting a decent-sized crowd to hear Shaw's advertised address. Though not a member of the League, he was already well regarded by most of its adherents, in whose eyes his reputation as an entertaining speaker excused his Fabian leanings. Despite disagreements about ways and means, George Bernard Shaw and William Morris shared a broad socialist goal. Shaw had contributed to *The Commonweal*, spoken at public meetings organised by the League, and earned Morris's esteem. It was quite evident, Lucy thought, that these two men respected each other's intellect and enjoyed a cordial friendship that could accommodate differences of political opinion and personal manner.

Letting the stream of conversation popple around her, she observed Shaw appraisingly. Like Morris, he seemed nonchalant about appearances. His crumpled clothes had a slept-in look, and that beard of his, fox-red and forking, was not carefully trimmed. The pale skin suggested ascetic habits. Yet his height and ramrod posture gave him a commanding presence while his gestures somehow blended affable self-confidence with a hint of shyness almost mastered. He spoke not only with his pleasant Irish brogue but with his body as well. His eyes gleamed mischievously as he shaped sentences into aphorisms. He had a way of throwing back his head to signal amusement, and liked slapping a fist into the palm of his other hand to emphasise a rhetorical point. She could see why May was captivated – though not deferential: while listening intently, her friend was disinclined to leave all the talking to the men, who at that moment were remarking on a report that cycling clubs had controversially begun to admit Lady Members.

May, wearing an impish expression, leant forward to interrupt. 'I hope you're not suggesting, Mr Shaw, that bicycles are suitable only for male riders. You've made some forthright statements elsewhere, I recall, in favour of equality for women.'

'I have indeed, Miss Morris. And just as it's my conviction' – he lifted an ironic eyebrow – 'that men no longer need special political privileges to protect them against women, so too their constant fear of being outshone by female prowess in any strenuous pursuit shouldn't mean that a beskirted person is denied the heady experience of mounting a rickety high-wheeler contraption to endanger herself and others.'

William Morris guffawed, May giggled, Lucy smiled.

Shaw went on in a more serious tone. 'Genuine equality for women – social, economic, political equality – may take much longer than we would wish. A few doors seem to be opening a chink: the Co-operative Movement is forming a Women's Guild, King's College London has established a Ladies Department, and I hear that even Oxford University now deigns to let female students take its entrance examination. But such little concessions touch very few. Wretched subordination remains the lot of most women.'

They all nodded. He's a clever performer, thought Lucy, as people began to arrive for the Socialist League meeting. Charmingly, disarmingly clever.

Before long, Shaw was beginning his address to the assembled group. He lifted his chin, drew in a deep breath that seemed to inflate his stature, and smiled at them all in a manner that combined buoyancy with a faintly sardonic detachment.

'Ladies and gentlemen, you know the saying that imitation is the sincerest form of flattery, but I beg to differ somewhat. There is surely an even purer grade of sincerity in self-quotation, a practice dear to my heart. When I manage to formulate anything that passes for wise and witty, I like to repeat it admiringly on other occasions. Some of you may be familiar with my provocative remark that the Established Government has no more right to call itself the State than the smoke of London has to call itself the weather. As this now strikes me as more apt than ever, I make it my starting point for tonight's talk...'

Two hours later, invigorated by Shaw's eloquence and the ensuing discussion, most of the League stalwarts had dispersed into the night. As Lucy was donning her dolman mantle and moving towards the door, May put a detaining hand on her arm and drew her aside. 'Don't leave without telling me what you think of him.'

'Ah!' Lucy twiddled with the buttons on a glove as she considered her impressions of the man. 'I'm sure most people would make the same remarks about Mr Shaw. His mind is exceptionally quick, isn't it? Sharp as a carving knife. He has a fine gift for coining irreverent phrases. Even people who might disagree with much of what he says could hardly ignore him.'

'But do you *like* him? And do you think he likes me?'

'Oh, he's likeable, certainly. And I've no doubt he holds you in high regard, May. The way he looks at you has something quietly affectionate in it. But not…well, one could hardly describe him as demonstrative. No great warmth in his manner, is there? He's keeping back a part of himself. There's some kind of physical reserve.'

'I fear you're right. Guarded towards women, as if telling himself not to be too masculine. It makes me want to startle him with an outburst of feeling, or at least with an oblique declaration that might tempt him to respond. I've half a mind to compose a hand-painted Valentine to send to him in February, some witty provocation, anonymous of course but with hints that he'd probably recognise. Should I try that?'

'I'm not the right person to ask, May. I know so little about men. They're completely opaque to me.'

'But you understand your Captain Kendrick pretty well, don't you?'

'No, I wouldn't say so.'

'Oh! Have I trodden carelessly? You're looking troubled. Do you want to talk about him?'

'Not now. It's late. I must be going.'

A few days later, at a secluded corner table in a South Kensington teashop, May broached the matter again.

'Has there been recent news from India? Something that's making you worried about Captain Kendrick?'

'A short letter came from him last week, saying his regiment was preparing to leave India. By now they'll be on their way to

Burma. Some conflict brewing there – he gave no details, but I suppose it could be a dangerous business.'

'Well, it's natural to be anxious about that. But when I asked about him after the League meeting in Hammersmith, you alluded to… What was it? Some misunderstanding between you?'

'Not quite a misunderstanding. More like a sprinkle of question marks. I just don't know what thoughts he may have about me, or about himself, if any. Perhaps he'd consider me similarly inscrutable, if he put his mind to pondering.'

'Is it always like that with soldiers, d'you think? For my part, I confess I can't fathom how the martial mind works. One of my father's brothers, Arthur, is a captain in the King's Royal Rifle Corps. He seems empty of any ideas except the most orthodox kind of manly patriotism. Went off to India himself a few years ago, and probably he's still stationed there – but might as well be on the moon for all the attention he seems to pay to the society of that exceedingly populous nation. To judge by his fitful correspondence with my father, there's little circulating in Uncle Arthur's noddle except a handful of bluff conventional phrases.'

'Nearly the same may be true of Julius Kendrick, for all I know.'

'Then what is it that attracts you?'

Lucy toyed with her teaspoon and shrugged. 'To be frank – I hope this won't shock you – I think it may be simply physical. On both sides.'

'Nothing shocking about carnal passion! He's a very handsome man, and you ought to feel gratified that someone so strongly masculine is drawn to you. What a contrast with Harry Sparling! Our League's new secretary. You met him at the meeting where

Shaw spoke, remember? You saw how Harry follows me around like a bespectacled puppy. His lovelorn attention embarrasses me because – unkind to say this, but it's the truth – he's just so unprepossessing! Thin, stooped and chinless.'

Lucy smiled. 'Poor Mr Sparling. But he does at least have an active brain. He thinks conscientiously about politics, about injustice, whereas Julius Kendrick is a man of action rather than of intellect. Intelligent, but not given to reflection and analysis, not a person who shows any sign of questioning the social order.' She lifted the teapot and then slowly put it down again as if having forgotten how to pour from it.

'When Kendrick is not with me,' she went on, 'I can see his limitations. I'm conscious of them as I try to compose replies to his letters, frowning over a squeaky nib. But when he's in my presence, he stirs something in me. Something…visceral – is that the word? Whether it's a stirring of curiosity or lust or fear, or an uneasy blend of all of these, I really can't be sure.'

In the ensuing silence Lucy's thoughts slipped sideways. The image of Captain Kendrick faded and another figure took his place, one that had sometimes stayed in the shadows but had never left her.

May spoke to her, and the memory dissolved instantly.

Writing from Rangoon in early November, Kendrick described the beginning of the Burmese campaign. An expeditionary force of nine thousand troops – a third British, the rest Indian – was being assembled in a flotilla to steam up the Irrawaddy. More than fifty armed naval paddleboats, he told Lucy, would tow these men upriver in lighters and barges. Their goal was to capture King Thibaw's royal capital of Ava, near Mandalay in upper Burma, and force his surrender.

By the time his letter reached her at the end of that month, she knew from a report in *The Times* that the conflict was already over: the speed of the British advance had surprised the Burmese, Mandalay had quickly fallen, the king had surrendered and the formalities of annexation would soon follow. There was some belated disquiet in England, a few questions being asked in parliament about the purpose of this invasion. But government voices insisted that Thibaw was a tyrant, that France had sought greater influence over Burma, and that imposing British rule delivered a benign solution to these problems. *The Commonweal* deplored the campaign: it was driven, Morris argued, by sheer greed for trading commodities such as teak and oil, and facilitated by the languid acquiescence of the public. Purporting to bestow the blessings of civilisation, it was actually violent robbery.

Another letter from Kendrick, dated 'Mandalay, Christmas Day 1885,' reached her in the New Year:

My dear Miss Malpass,
Our regiment is now quartered outside the city walls in Buddhist monasteries, called Phoongyee Kyoungs, which must be the brightest barracks ever occupied by British troops. In the sunlight these strange edifices are ablaze with gold leaf and fragments of glass. Their pagan builders could not have imagined that one day British soldiers would be singing 'Hark the Herald Angels' in such a place. Divine service this morning was conducted in the open air outside one of the buildings, our men being fully armed on parade as we never know when an alarm might be sounded.

We are very glad to have a day's rest because our occupation of Mandalay is a tense business. Although our victory was swiftly proclaimed, there is still sporadic resistance from bandits ('dacoits' is the local word) who lurk in the surrounding jungle and creep into parts of the city to harry us. This whole expedition has been more difficult than we had imagined. Coming up the river we were under fire from stockades on both sides, and then after disembarking we had to march through thick jungle before we could attack some of the forts. Our uniforms made us an easy target, and are not well suited to this steamy climate. It's hard to keep the spirits up when everyone is sweat-soaked and grimy. I won't go into any detail about the fighting itself. You can imagine it was gruesome, with bayonet charges and hand-to-hand combat, not for the faint-hearted. Barton and I acquitted ourselves pretty well, and our commander Major-General Prendergast says we have both been mentioned in despatches – which, you know, is quite a feather in one's cap!

There was a little more in the same vein, with only a perfunctory enquiry at the end about her welfare. Were all men so self-pre-occupied? So blithely sure that wherever they happened to be standing was at that moment the centre of the world?

During the months that followed, correspondence from Kendrick became intermittent and lethargic. Dacoits were continuing to harass British outposts, he wrote, and this would require him with some of his regiment to stay on indefinitely, attempting to quell the episodic insurgency around Mandalay. There had been occasional flurries of action but also long periods of boredom. He was whiling away much of the time playing cards with his foster-brother Gerard Barton and two other officers. He could think of little to report that would be of any interest to her.

As 1886 came towards its close, Kendrick had still made no mention of returning to England. She felt slighted. Too proud to disclose a sense of injury, she had resorted to reciprocal neglect, letting her letters to him dwindle. Her heart was drooping. She no longer took much pleasure in anything now, even in her needlework at Merton Abbey. A moulting bird might feel like this, she imagined – sulky, wishing only to avoid company.

Then, in the last week of the year, a brief but perturbing letter came to her from Burma – sent by someone else.

Dear Miss Malpass

No doubt you will be surprised at my presumption in writing to you. I do so only after arguing conscientiously with myself as to whether it is proper to communicate in this way, in view of your special friendship with my foster-brother Julius. He is not aware of this letter.

Our regiment, as you know, has been stationed here for more than a year. Despite what you may have been led to believe, individual officers are not obliged to remain here beyond this time. Although skirmishes will probably continue around Mandalay for a little longer, the situation is generally under control. Those of us in senior ranks are now able to apply, if we wish, for a period of extended leave. Having done so, I expect to be back in England before long. Julius, alas, says he has no plan to return home in the foreseeable future.

I trust that you are in good health. It is my intention to visit you as soon as I disembark. There are things to tell you that it would not be fitting to divulge in a letter.

Meanwhile I remain

Yours very respectfully,

Gerard Barton

Swindon
1887-89

THIRTEEN

ARLY IN THE NEW YEAR, BARTON ARRIVED AT HER DOOR in person. Until now she had paid little attention to him. He had been Kendrick's associate, hardly more. Now, as he talked on at length in the drawing room of her De Vere Gardens flat, an earnest intensity suffusing everything he said, she observed closely his features and comportment.

Gerard Barton was tall, almost as tall as Kendrick, and solidly built. He sat bolt upright in the armchair, resolutely maintaining a soldier's bearing. His hair and whiskers were the colour of pale straw. Except for a broad fleshy nose and uneven teeth, he was moderately handsome. While he spoke he gazed at her intently, fire flickering in his eyes.

It was a long passionate monologue. He told her about his upbringing, adopted by the neighbouring Kendrick family from the age of six after the smallpox carried off his parents; about his close relationship with Julius, his elder by a year; about their shared choice of an army career; about the mostly tedious time in India, and then the initial elation and later tensions of the Burma campaign; and about their recent falling-out.

'We began to argue over his use of opium, which army orders strictly forbid. He turns to it, on the sly, more and more often. Although he manages to hide what he's doing from other senior officers, I know him well enough to see how it's changing him for the worse. He's become not only secretive but also moody. Much of the time a kind of lethargy settles on him, punctuated by bursts of anger.'

Barton gave a long sigh, and paused to sip the tea that she had just poured for him. 'There's something more,' he went on. 'I've been hesitant about revealing this but I believe you have a right to know it. I regret to say that Julius has become fond of a Burmese woman, a pretty almond-coloured girl, a cheroot-maker. How deeply his feelings are engaged I can't say, though she is clearly enamoured of him, and it's likely she's the person who has been supplying him with opium. Be that as it may, he now seems incapable of making sensible decisions. It's only a matter of time before his behaviour comes to the notice of his superiors, and then he'll probably be charged with dereliction of duty. For some weeks I made every effort to protect him from discovery, but eventually I spoke to him in forthright terms about his folly. I told him that by dawdling in Burma he had surely jeopardised the prospect of securing your affections. I urged him to return to England even if it might mean relinquishing his military career, and to seek your agreement to marry him. But despite my entreaties, Julius refuses to make a decisive move. He continues to float along in an opium haze, and there's now a wall of vexation between us.'

'It's deeply troubling to hear all of this,' said Lucy, her voice faint. Half-formed questions began to buzz around the things he had told her, but she wasn't yet able to put them into words.

'What I've already said is much more than you would have wanted to hear, no doubt,' said Barton. 'Nevertheless I feel bound to mention one other matter before I go. I hope this statement won't be unwelcome, Miss Malpass. It's about my own feelings. My feelings towards you. I've always carried a torch for you, and I'm asking you to let me show, in time, that I can be a loyal and devoted companion.'

Taken aback, Lucy sat in silence with her head bent down. She could sense that he was waiting for a response, but distress and confusion clogged her throat, impeding words. Several minutes went by before he rose stiffly, murmured an apology, and left the room.

Winter gave way to early signs of spring, and still nothing came from Captain Kendrick. She could not bring herself to write to him.

Barton became a frequent caller at her flat. A couple of times he tried to renew his declaration, but when he approached the subject she shook her head and raised her hand in a hushing gesture.

Heart-to-heart talks with May brought no equanimity. While frank in her avowals, Lucy remained irresolute.

'It's clear that I've lost Kendrick,' she told her friend during one of these intimate discussions. 'Yet when I lie down at night, his shadow lies beside me and touches my body.'

'Then shouldn't you write to him and tell him so? At least let him know what Barton says about him, and give him a chance to explain himself?'

'No, I won't do that. Even if the picture Barton has drawn is misrepresenting Kendrick, the simple fact remains that it's months now since I had a letter from him. For me to write to him after such neglect would be tantamount to pleading for his attention, and I refuse to make myself a figure of pathos.'

'Perhaps it would break the spell he seems to be under.'

'I'm the one who's under a spell, but I mustn't allow him to him know that he has such a hold over me. Even if he were to appear on my doorstep tomorrow, begging forgiveness and vowing fidelity, I'd turn him away.'

'Well then, Lucy... What's to be done? Do you intend to shut yourself away from male companionship altogether, just because one man treats you in an uncouth way? If you're determined to have nothing further to do with Kendrick, must you continue to repel Lieutenant Barton too? He's an amiable fellow, is he not? And seems devoted to you.'

Lucy shrugged, and the topic lapsed. But in the ensuing weeks she continued to mull it over wearily. One midsummer day, on a capricious impulse, she yielded to Barton's repeated appeals.

'Yes,' she told him suddenly. 'Yes, I will marry you.'

His boyish delight was boundless until a letter from his foster-father made it plain that this wedding could not be the sociable event Barton had naively envisaged. His plan – to marry Lucy in a village church near the country estate where he had grown up, in northwest Hampshire, and to celebrate with a gathering afterwards in his adoptive family's home – met with a curt and cold parental rejection.

'Oh, I should have anticipated this rupture,' he told Lucy dejectedly. 'I'd written to Julius some weeks ago, you see – I felt duty bound to do so – letting him know that I wanted to marry you. He hasn't replied to me but no doubt he sent a furious letter to our parents about it. Evidently they've sided with him. He would have represented my action as treacherous, I'm sure, despite the fact that he has treated you in such a neglectful way – a virtual abandonment – and is still dilly-dallying in Burma.'

They wed inconspicuously in Winchester, with no guests present except May Morris, and began their married life by briefly renting a cottage, cramped and unsewered, at the edge of the town.

'Although it's a far cry from your relinquished flat in De Vere Gardens, this comedown is quite temporary,' Barton assured her. 'As soon as I've found a suitable farm property to purchase, I can arrange through my lawyer to draw on the substantial inheritance left in trust when my parents died, my real parents.'

'Farm?'

'Yes. I've had enough of soldiering. Dairy farming is what I want to do now. I'll be looking for a good piece of land, probably across the county border, up in the northern part of Wiltshire.'

'But Gerard, I wouldn't relish the role of a farmer's wife any more than the role of a soldier's wife! You don't expect me to milk cows?'

'No no, of course not. I'll appoint a manager to supervise the business of the farm, and he'll hire farmhands for the day-to-day work.'

A couple of months later Barton bought a freehold property near Stratton St Margaret, a large piece of well-tended arable land that would lend itself readily to conversion from cropping to pasture.

'It's an excellent location,' he told her enthusiastically. 'There's a new milk depot nearby, and a railway station for quick distribution of churns into London. I'll stock the place with a herd of Shorthorn cattle. They give good yields. I can sell whey to a pig breeder just half a mile away. And I'll have a large skilling built.'

'A skilling?'

'That's the name for a cowshed around these parts.'

'Ah.' Lucy smiled. 'Not for us to live in, then?'

'We can certainly do better than that, my dear.'

With their combined resources they bought a large villa near the railway station in New Swindon, a few miles from their acreage. All the little practical aspects of setting up house helped to distract Lucy from facing the large implications of her choice to marry Gerard. It was too soon to let herself think about how she would adjust to the abandoning of her Merton Abbey employment or the loss of people whose lives had long been entwined with hers, particularly her loyal retainer Perkins – now retiring to Leek – and her closest confidante, May.

While Gerard travelled each day to confer with his farm manager on everything from constructing sheds to acquiring livestock, she busied herself with various domestic tasks. It took some while to hire a suitable housekeeper, to find out which merchants in the town could be relied upon, to select wallpaper and fabrics and furniture. In quiet daylight hours at her window seat she embroidered cushions and a bedspread. Of an evening, while Gerard smoked an after-dinner cigar and read the newspaper, she often wrote to May about the textiles and threads she had selected, or the details of patterns she was devising or adapting. May's letters to her reported on the latest projects at the Merton Abbey works, the latest debates among Socialist League members, and the latest knot in her skein of exasperated feelings about Bernard Shaw.

Since leaving London, Lucy had found it difficult to travel regularly to Ticehurst, especially with the distractions of her wedding and new domestic arrangements. She continued to send letters to her forlornly sequestered aunt, trusting that a conscientious nurse would have the patience to read them aloud to her. Several weeks after moving into the New Swindon villa she told her husband that she wanted to visit the asylum again. He would prefer to accompany her, he said, but must attend the local mid-week cattle market. Could she wait until after that? No, it was high time for her to visit her aunt, and she would go alone. She was accustomed to railway journeys and found most of them agreeable. This time, as she would be changing trains in London, she might take an additional day or two there on the way back, extending her absence into what people were now calling 'the weekend' so that she could spend a few hours with May Morris.

She found her aunt in an even feebler, more bewildered condition than before. Unable to utter intelligible words, Barbara Brodie gurgled like an infant while making fluttery gestures with her frail hands.

'You poor dear,' said Lucy. 'I do hope you're not in any pain. Perhaps you can't comprehend anything I say, but a monologue seems better than silence. So I'll just speak freely about what's on my mind, and even if it makes little sense to you there's no harm done.'

Her aunt's hand gave a twitch, or little wave, which could have been intended as encouragement. Or not.

'In fact, Aunt, I don't always make much sense to myself, that's the absurd truth. I often think one thing but say or do something quite different. Especially in my dealings with men. You were right to tell me, a long while ago, that I treated Captain Kendrick unreasonably. I don't quite know why I was so capricious and rejecting, except that I felt… oh, in danger of letting myself be overwhelmed, I suppose. Alarmed by the passions he stirred up in me. In my mind. And in my flesh, to be candid. So I held him at bay. But then he went off into the far distance, and stayed away from me, irked or disheartened or…I don't know…I thought, I probably thought, that he would persist, and go on pleading until I composed myself enough to admit…to open the door to him. But it didn't happen.'

Barbara Brodie had begun to dribble and make whimpering noises. Lucy wiped her aunt's chin.

'And then his friend, his foster-brother… You remember Lieutenant Gerard Barton? He saw the rift widen, made it into an opportunity, and now all of a sudden I'm his wife, and I shouldn't be. He's a decent man and does his utmost to please me, but what I feel for him, the gratitude, the affectionate respect – it's nothing like the disturbing mixture of emotions that Julius Kendrick kindled in me.'

Lucy's voice had risen, and seemed still to resound through the little room for a few moments after she stopped speaking. With a worried frown, she stared at her aunt, whose limbs and face were becoming increasingly agitated. Then, with a groan, the bent body uncurled, pitched forward and lay sprawled on the floor, inert.

Within a few hours Dr Hayes Newington had completed the death certificate and arranged for the chaplain to conduct a simple burial service the following afternoon. Lucy spent the night at small hotel in Tunbridge Wells, bought suitable mourning attire in the town the next day, and returned by carriage to Ticehurst.

As the chaplain droned on, she reflected wryly that her aunt, too, would have found his sentimental piety and sanctimonious tone tiresome. For Barbara Brodie, as for Lucy herself, religious observance was never more than perfunctory. In Leek, with her young niece in tow, she had dutifully attended matins at their parish church, St Edward's; but she did so, Lucy knew, partly for aesthetic reasons, there being much to appreciate in the fine decorative details of that dignified structure, and partly for the sake of social comfort. To flout certain expectations in a small provincial town would be verging on the scandalous. Privately, in Lucy's hearing, Mrs Brodie often made ironic comments on what she liked to call 'ecclesiastical pomposity.' After moving to London, they both gave up churchgoing without needing to discuss the matter. Lucy had derived from her father a similarly sceptical cast of mind: Henry Malpass turned away sharply from the blandishments of religion when his wife and son died. During her Leek days Lucy took care not to be provocatively irreligious in the company of devout neighbours such as the Wardles. Besides, she was unfeigned in admiring the Embroidery Society's meticulously worked altar cloths and priestly vestments. What did it matter that a set of beliefs was merely superstitious, if it could still create such beautiful things? When sitting in a pew of their church, she paid little attention to sermons or rituals. Her eyes would linger on cherished design features within the building: the contrasting roof timber patterns in the nave and chancel, the sparkling play of colours in the imposing glass windows, the balance of marble with alabaster in the font, the elegant carvings around the dark wooden pulpit.

As soon as the dreary little burial service was over, she made brisk arrangements for the disposal of her aunt's effects, thanked Newington for his kindly care, and left Ticehurst. Travelling back westward, she could not quell the voice in her head that repeated the same painful truths she had been expressing at the moment when her aunt expired. She was now on her way home, home in New Swindon, where the house that she had been so assiduously furnishing and the husband who had been so solicitously providing for her awaited her return – and she did not want to be there.

Like May, whose most recent letter revealed that she was now contemplating marriage to the previously disdained Henry Sparling, Lucy had turned to someone other than the person with whom she longed to be. Though Gerard was a good man and a diligent lover, her feelings for him were not passionate. Often at night, as he moved on top of her and drew her body into a crescendo of carnal rhythms, she tried to imagine it was Julius Kendrick pulsing inside her. She had wedded Gerard on a foolish impulse, punishing herself for having wounded the relationship with Julius. She seldom thought about Gerard, even when in the same room with him, but Julius was never far from her mind.

She supposed she would never see him again.

FOURTEEN

O NE SOMBRE AFTERNOON OF LOWERING CLOUD, AS LUCY was coming out of a drapery shop in Swindon's Regent Street, someone tall loomed in front of her. Startled, glancing up, she saw that it was Julius Kendrick. She clapped a hand to her heart. He lifted his hat and inclined his head. His skin looked sallow, his once lustrous eyes dull, pink-rimmed.

'Captain...' she began to say, and stopped. It seemed too formal, and besides, he was not in military uniform. 'Or have you left...?'

'Resigned my commission a few months ago, after finally admitting that Burma had become poisonous to my spirit.'

'That sounds melodramatic. What do you mean?'

'Oh, I've no doubt Barton has already painted a dark enough portrait. I'll spare you any pleading about excuses. The upshot is that I came to my senses eventually, but too late, I'm afraid, to regain your trust.'

Her eyes avoided his.

'Whatever brings you to Swindon?' she asked, glancing along the unlovely street.

'I heard you live here now. So I thought that by staying for a few days at a local inn I'd have a chance of happening to see you in the town sooner or later, and be able to speak to you.'

'Why not call on us at home?'

'I'll have nothing to do with Barton. It's only with you that I wish to talk.'

Bemused, she looked around. 'Here? In the street?'

'This will do as well as anywhere else. I won't take much of your time. There's very little to say, but I must say it now, while I can.'

Apprehensive, she pressed her hands together and waited. She could smell rum on his breath.

'Lucy,' he faltered. 'Lucy…' Then, breathing in deeply, he went on. 'The news of your marriage dismayed me. No, much more than that: it devastated me utterly. I don't reproach you, of course. I shouldn't have let myself be so easily rebuffed before leaving for India. I was certain your feelings towards me ran deeper than you were acknowledging. So I ought to have been more insistent, more steadfast. Somehow I drifted into a long stupor, a kind of heartsickness, and just couldn't bring myself to explain in my letters what was happening to me. Too proud, or too ashamed, or a muddle of both. For that failure the blame is mine entirely.'

She began to murmur something in response, but he stopped her with a gesture and continued speaking. A tone of urgency permeated every phrase.

'I know how culpable I am. But I do feel angry towards Barton. Intensely, bitterly aggrieved. He knew full well that my feelings for you were undimmed, that I just needed time to pull myself out of the torpid state I'd lapsed into. He took advantage of the situation, and I can't forgive him. He's been no friend to me in this matter. I don't regard him any longer as my brother. But I'll always think of you, dear Lucy, as the woman who should have become my wife, if not for my foolish inaction and his treachery.'

A scatter of raindrops began to fall. She pointed her umbrella at the pewter sky.

There was so much she wanted to say to him, entangled in a jumble of emotions that she could name in general terms but not unravel. Remorse was part of it, twisted up with resentments, longings, frustrations...

Holding back tears, she was unable to speak. At length he turned away and she stood there in misery, watching him walk slowly down the street through the drizzle into a hopeless distance.

To Gerard she said nothing about the disturbing encounter. In the following days, when he remarked on how pallid she looked, she told him it was nothing more than a slight indisposition. A few weeks later she became sure of something which, though she privately thought it unconnected with her listless mood, would seem to Gerard a complete explanation and a wonderful piece of news. She was, she told him softly, with child.

To all the future practicalities of giving birth and rearing a child she gave little thought. Time enough later for that. Meanwhile she would carry on as if nothing had changed, though this was plainly not her husband's attitude. The prospect of fatherhood made him even more attentive to her than before. Almost comically uxorious, she thought.

'I'm not fragile, Gerard!' she protested as he hovered and fussed around her. 'The fact that my belly is gradually swelling doesn't make me an invalid!'

'But you should get plenty of rest, my dear.'

'I can't just sit around the house all day, month after month. Such boredom! It stifles me.'

So at her insistence he took her out 'for an airing' – a little excursion through the handsome adjacent village of Stratton St Margaret and on further to see the improvements being made on their farm property. The weather was tranquil, the sky clear, her mind untouched by the faintest quiver of foreboding.

Their carriage took them along one of the dusty farm roads past new and modified outbuildings, on past fenced pastures freshly stocked with large dairy herds, towards a small paddock where he wanted to show her his recent acquisition, a brawny roan bull.

'The size of the brute!' Gerard exclaimed with pride. 'Look at the thick shoulders on him, and those haunches. He'll be a lusty breeder.'

'Strange mix of colouring, isn't it? His front half is nearly all deep red-brown, like our big mahogany table, but the hindquarters look as if someone has splashed a bucket of whitewash over them.'

'Quite common with Shorthorns, that pattern.'

'It's an odd name for the breed. Look at those ferocious horns! Isn't it usual for bulls to be polled, anyway?'

'In this breed, some cattle develop horns, others never do. The idea of polling a mature horned bull doesn't appeal to me at all. I think this one is really quite magnificent in his natural state. Let's take a closer look.'

Dismounting from their carriage, they walked over to the fence. Lucy rested her hand on her rounded midriff. The bull stared at them, nostrils twitching, and ambled in their direction. Rubbed its flank rhythmically along the wooden gate. Made rumbling sounds that grew louder and turned into a series of raucous bugle-like blasts. Then it began to rock sideways, to and fro, with increasing force, until its whole massive body was thumping and crashing against the gate, rattling the timber planks, which now seemed alarmingly flimsy. Lucy backed away. There was a sudden cracking, splintering noise. The gate jerked loose and lurched back from its post. Lucy and Gerard scrambled towards their carriage but the beast came at them fast, tossing its head, snorting. Lucy tripped, and although Gerard tried desperately to help her to her feet it was upon them, its monstrous head now lowered, thrusting a horn into Lucy's belly and flicking her contemptuously aside before charging on down the path away from them with puffs of dust in its wake.

It was astonishing, people said during her long convalescence, how anyone could survive being gored so badly. Steady recovery now seemed assured: what a marvel! To Lucy this refrain was so irksome that she had to clench her teeth to stop herself from crying out in exasperation at hearing yet again about her 'miraculous' escape from death's door, especially as the sentiment had a pious tone. Not at all, she wanted to insist, what had saved her wasn't any divine intervention. It was the new antiseptic surgical method established by Sir Joseph Lister. When dressings were being changed she forced herself to look at the fearsome wound in her abdomen. To the expert eye of a needlework artist there was nothing delicate in the stitches binding its jagged edges, but she knew that if it hadn't been for the surgeon's use of carbolic catgut as a sterile suturing thread she might not be alive.

Chatter about the wonder of her survival annoyed her for a deeper reason as well: she was achingly aware of all that had not survived. After recovering from the temporary physical losses – an almost fatal outpouring of blood and a long comatose erasure of consciousness – she saw them as trivial compared with what was now gone forever: not only her unborn child but also any possibility of bearing further children. To this profound bereavement an accumulation of previous losses adhered. Her aunt's death repeated that of her parents. The relinquishing of companionable employment at the Merton Abbey works diminished her sense of vocation as an embroiderer. The move away from London meant she could no longer be part of the Morris circle. And her wanton slighting of Julius forfeited the prospect of any future with him.

While Lucy lay stricken on her bed, febrile at first and then enfeebled, the months dragging by, May Morris came twice to see her. 'I dearly wish I could visit more often, or stay with you for a time,' she said, 'but everything is so frantic just now at Merton Abbey, with orders overdue and certain fabrics hard to obtain and looms to be repaired…'

May brought condolences from family and friends, gossip about Socialist League members, and news that the Bayeux Tapestry replica brilliantly stitched by ladies of the Leek Embroidery Society was now on display in London. She also brought a gift – 'for you to read when your health returns': a copy of her father's long narrative poem *The Lovers of Gudrun*, retold from an Icelandic saga. Feeling too weak to give it any close attention, Lucy languidly turned a few pages and then put the book aside for later reading.

From drooping lethargy her mood would swing into surges of anger, often provoked by her husband's fumbling contrition for having failed to protect her from danger on the farm. The more apologetic Gerard became, the more his presence annoyed her. She brushed his words aside and dismissed him from her bedside. Emotionally he's a simpleton, she thought.

Almost a year after the accident, her body now healed but her spirit still frail, Lucy received from Julius Kendrick a letter that would have dark consequences.

It had just come to his hearing, he wrote, that she sustained a serious injury some time ago; and though she was now reportedly recovering well, he wished to send his sympathy and express concern for her welfare. He didn't know whether what he had been told about the circumstances of her mishap was a reliable account; but if a person who ought to have been a steadfast protector had indeed exposed her needlessly to jeopardy, this would be deplorable.

He went on to mention something else, something that shocked her into such a fit of tearful fury that she hurled her hairbrush at a mirror, sending slivers of glass tinkling across the bedroom floor. Julius was now married, and his wife was expecting a child.

Ill-tempered agitation roiled within her for days before turning into a different kind of derangement, hard and implacable. Kendrick's letter solidified the distress that had stayed with her since she last saw him. Time and again her mind repeated their clumsy conversation in the street. His remembered words had become shards of gravel glinting on the bed of a cold stream. Did he think that by confessing his 'drift into a stupor' he might earn her forgiveness? He was too sorry for himself to understand how he had made her suffer. Her marriage had 'dismayed' him, had it? Well, the blame was certainly all his. He had driven her into his foster-brother's arms. If not for his own self-absorption and all that protracted dawdling in Burma, she could have been married to him and would never have made the impulsive decision to turn to Gerard Barton, never have thought of becoming a farmer's wife, never have gone near that hideous bull.

She let whole days pass in a mopey silence. Though Barton kept expressing concern about her withdrawn mood, Lucy made no response at first. In her mind she was haranguing him with phrases just as vehement as those she'd imagined hurling at Kendrick, but she pursed her lips for as long as she could. When he persisted with his fluttering questions, something akin to madness seized her and she began to tell him frankly what she felt. Holding little back, she spoke with a directness that was shocking even to herself, and dazed Gerard.

He sat submissively, head bowed, as her bitter words buffeted him. It wasn't only the accident on the farm, she told him. Her whole future had been grievously injured. Miserable? Of course she was miserable! Cut off from her friends and activities in London, she was mouldering away here in this dull Wiltshire town, slowly rotting in a slough of utter boredom. She had married the wrong man – that was the blunt truth. She was sorry to have to say so, and sorrier still to have made such a blundering mistake. Barton deserved a better wife, yet she simply could not make herself into that person by an effort of will. In a flat tone that belied the ache beneath her words, and with a candour that she knew was cruel but could not repress, she went on to mention the welter of emotions that his foster-brother Kendrick had aroused in her: the suppressed passion, the furious resentment, the desolation.

Swindon 1887–89

Lucy fell silent for a few minutes, not looking at her husband, and then quickly stood up and left the room. Though aware that what she had disclosed would hurt him deeply, she could not help it. Her own soul felt bruised beyond repair.

FIFTEEN

*T*HE DAY HAD TURNED BRIGHT AND WARM, BUT LUCY paid no heed to that. She sat indoors, staring blankly at a featureless wall, which might as well have been a window through which nothing was visible but a prospect of infinite greyness. For a couple of hours she had remained in the same chair, a book unopened on her lap, her thoughts wandering disconsolately. The whole house was as silent as a snowdrift. Their young servant, Stead, had the day off to visit her cousin in Chippenham. Gerard, worried about the falling market price of milk, was in town to ask his banker for an extension of loan arrangements. Lucy had expected him back before now, but was glad of the delay. Retreating into solitude felt much easier these days than making strained conversation.

Sensing Lucy's low spirits, Stead had lingered before departing for her day's leave, and ventured a hesitant comment. 'Perhaps it's not my place to say so, Ma'am, but you haven't been yourself lately, that's the truth of it. I don't like to see you pining away in here. A bit of company would cheer you up, it would.'

Lucy had demurred. No, she just didn't feel up to talking with anyone at present, but this was not a cause for worry. And no, really, there was nothing Stead could do for her before setting out. A day at home would pass satisfactorily in quiet reflection and reading. So with an acquiescent nod, Stead left her to it.

Her watchful servant, Lucy knew, would be well aware that the household had become unhappy, that husband and wife seldom exchanged more than a few words at a time, and that the primary fault was not his. Though he had his shortcomings, Lucy could hardly blame him for the tensions that now hung in the space between them. What had gone wrong with their marriage stemmed mostly from her own foolish acceptance of his proposal – and from the previous fact of Kendrick's inertia, which had enabled Barton to slide into the vacated suitor's role. Desiring to be her husband was no crime on his part; agreeing to be his wife when she did not desire it made her the guilty one. She felt sorry for him, vexed with herself, and unsure what to do next.

A rat-tat-tat resounded from the front door knocker. She would have to answer it herself. But who could this be? Not Gerard – he always let himself in. Not, she hoped, their intrusive neighbour Miss Susanna Spinks, a self-appointed monitor of Lucy's convalescence, who often had the whim of coaxing her into a stroll along the street 'for one's health's sake, my dear.'

Opening the door, she saw a ghost swaying on the steps – tall, dark and tipsy. She was struck speechless.

Kendrick doffed his hat. 'Mrs Barton. Won't you ask me to come in?' There was an indistinct hiss in 'ask': drink, apparently, had half-numbed his tongue.

Still saying nothing, she pulled the door wider and stepped back to imply an invitation, though without any welcoming warmth. There was a tumult in her head, a hammer in her chest. He followed her into the drawing room as she tried to compose herself.

'Forgive me,' he said as they sat down, 'for coming here unannounced, on an impulse. Happened to observe your husband enter a commercial building in the town, and thought I might find you at home while he's occupied there.'

In his face she could see traces of dissipation and lines of discontentment. His complexion had the colour of a tallow candle. Her own skin, she supposed, was also pallid and worn now. She made an effort to steady her breathing.

'It's a long while since I last saw you,' she said. 'The time when you accosted me in the street here. Why are you in Swindon again?'

'Oh, just a bizjness' – he stumbled over the word – '…business matter. My wife's parents are having difficulties with a property investment here. Ashked me to get advice about it on their behalf from a local lawyer. I came up this morning from Winchester. Thass where we live now. Return there this evening.'

The mention of his wife had made Lucy wince. Did he notice this? Unlikely, she thought. He was glancing now around the thickly curtained room, seemingly at a loss to know what to say next. His gaze came to rest on her.

'You did get the letter I sent after hearing about your accident?'

She nodded.

He pressed on. 'But didn't reply.'

'What could I say? You'd hardly expect me, in the circumstances, to congratulate you on your marriage and prospective fatherhood?'

Her sharp tone made him jerk his face away as if she had slapped it, but he persevered.

'I hoped…hoped you would reassure me you were fully recovered. Having heard nothing, I decided to come here and see for myself whether all is well. As appears to be the case. You are looking…looking particularly…'

As he searched for a suitable word, she interjected bitterly: 'Looking? But I can't *look forward* to anything I want! Especially not to any *children*, unlike you and your *wife!*'

She saw that her flaring resentment had scorched him.

'I'm sorry to hear it,' he murmured, eyes down. 'More sorry than I know how to express.' The old erect bearing had left him. His posture now embodied something she hadn't seen in him before. Could it be compunction? Contrition?

She drew back from the emotions she had momentarily let loose, affecting now an insouciant air, lifting her shoulders and opening her hands as she spoke. 'Oh, childlessness may be for the best. I probably lack the qualities needed in a good parent.'

But what kind of mother, she wondered, would his wife be? What kind of person was she? How had he met her? Lucy didn't permit herself to ask any of the things she was burning to know. He glanced at her uncertainly, looked away, and folded his hands.

The room had become a pool of deep silence except for the clock's drip-drip.

'Despite everything that's happened since,' he began, and then wavered and came to a stop. He tried again. 'Through all of it, I've often thought back fondly to the afternoon of our first encounter. That exuberant tea dance. The quadrilles, the waltzes. Our tentative conversation. Remember?'

How could she forget any of it? Everything experienced that day, so many years ago, was still imprinted indelibly on her mind. Admiring his comportment, feeling his voice enter her as he sang, being on her guard when they first talked, and then moving rhythmically with him through those formal patterns of steps – all the details had stayed with her. But simultaneously his mention of dancing perturbed her, too, and she half-knew why: it touched a deeper, troubling layer of memory. Shoving aside this incipient recognition, she answered acerbically: 'There's little comfort in a few sentimental memories.'

He stood up and moved unsteadily towards her chair.

'But there's great harm in denying how those remembered emotions shape our lives. Won't you acknowledge…'

As he stretched a hand towards her, Lucy was seized by a fit of tearful shouting. Acknowledge! How dare he, how dare he implore her to acknowledge feelings that he himself had failed to express, let alone act upon, during all that wasteful time in India! He'd neglected her, slighted her, put his soldiering ahead of his pledges to her, let himself lapse into a long narcotic and alcoholic daydream, given her eventually no real choice but to yield to Gerard's advances, to accept an outcome she hadn't wanted and shouldn't have permitted… The tirade went on, a snarl of twisted threads, reproachful, remorseful, anguished.

He stood there, letting her angry words flog him, as if by submitting to this onslaught he might share some of the unexpressed feeling he saw behind it. And then, suddenly, he stepped forward and caught her by the shoulders, wishing to gather up all their misery and fold it into a receptive embrace.

Head flung back, she squirmed in his arms and pushed her fists against his chest, another surge of rage mingling with heartsick desperation.

Just as she released a wailing cry there was a noise of rapid footfalls in the hallway and Barton burst into the room, brandishing a knobbed walking cane. He ran over to them and yanked them apart. Lucy staggered away, her frame shaken with sobs. As she leant against the wall she saw the two men fall together to the floor, wrestling furiously, punching, threshing. Then Kendrick spat out blood and oaths, grasped a table leg and hauled himself upright. At the same moment Barton stood quickly, snatching up the heavy stick that he had dropped. He swung it around and struck Kendrick hard on the temple. As Kendrick toppled back, his head hit the table edge with a loud crack. He slumped to the ground, twitching, and then lay still. Blood oozed, spreading around his face and forming a pool.

Transfixed with incredulity, Lucy wrapped her arms around her belly and made little low moaning sounds. Barton knelt for a moment beside his foster-brother, but then, seeing that the prone figure was utterly lifeless, he dropped back into an armchair and sat there in a daze, his trembling hands over his face. Lucy went on whimpering. It was a long while before either could find any shape for any words.

Hands in a penitential clasp, head bowed, voice hardly more than a whisper, Barton began to mumble, apparently to himself or even to the corpse rather than to her. She heard a few faint phrases: he seemed to be sinking into a lament for what had been extinguished long before the striking of this deadly blow: the love of brother for brother. After a few minutes his murmuring slowed and trailed off. He turned towards her in what seemed to be some kind of mute appeal.

A question squeezed its way out of her throat. 'Why, Gerard?'

He looked dumbfounded. 'Why? Why did I strike him? Because he was assaulting you! I heard your screams as I approached the house, and then, when I came running in, there you were – my wife struggling with an intruder! I didn't recognise who it was at first, and of course I didn't mean to kill him, but he had to be stopped! If I hadn't arrived when I did… He was intent on… God knows – rape! Or murder! '

'No! Not so! I was distraught and he was trying to comfort me. It's true I was crying out, because I wouldn't let myself be comforted, but he wasn't to blame. He meant me no harm. You're the murderer!'

Aghast, he stared at her. 'But I didn't want Julius dead! You must know that! You were under attack, calling out in distress, and I was simply protecting you!' He stood suddenly and began to pace up and down. 'I'll have to go to the police at once. Explain how this terrible thing happened.' He turned to her, his face suffused with consternation. 'You will confirm, won't you, Lucy, that I wasn't at fault?'

She couldn't bring herself to reply. Her whole body was shaking. She wept and wept.

By the time Gerard left their house to report the death, Lucy had impulsively made a crucial decision. She would not stay here any longer. Could not. Unfair though it might be to desert him when he was relying on her testimony to exculpate him, and rash though she knew this might later seem, she must leave immediately. It wasn't a question of blame. To go on living in this place with this man after what he had just done, and after all else that had happened, had simply become an unbearable prospect.

Quickly she packed a few clothes into Gerard's new Gladstone bag, filled a purse with money, and set off on foot. It would take her only a few minutes to reach the station where the regular evening train for London was due to depart before sunset. She would write later to Gerard and to Stead.

There were not many people in the streets as she hurried towards the railway building, and she was glad of this, not wanting to have to explain to any acquaintance where she was going and why. Nor did she have time to linger. She ignored a beggar woman crouching on the footpath and stepped around a noisy group of boys playing hopscotch. Two straw-hatted young men swept past her on penny-farthings, obviously well pleased with their elevated pose, and she recalled Bernard Shaw's droll remark about the heady experience of being atop such a rickety contraption.

Although the evening train was unlikely to be crowded, she would avoid first-class carriages, the probable choice of anyone she knew who might happen to be travelling at this time. With luck a second-class compartment would afford her some privacy so that she could put her thoughts in order and decide what exactly to do in London. So far she had conceived no more than a vague idea of asking May Morris for help with temporary accommodation and for advice on how and where to start a new life. She was trying not to acknowledge the qualms now plucking at her, not to permit herself any second thoughts about the haste of this sudden flight from Swindon, from her marriage, from respectability and material comfort.

As there was no queue, buying her ticket took only a few moments. Then she went straight into the second-class waiting room and sat in a dimly lit corner. She would probably feel faint with hunger by the time she reached London, but the refreshment room here did not tempt her; the train from Bath was about to make its requisite ten-minute stop, disgorging a boisterous jostle of passengers in a rush to quench their thirst and appease their appetite before they had to board again. The thought of swarming crowds was as distasteful to her as a gristle-filled pork pie or a bowl of tepid soup. She avoided the bookstall too, having previously put in her bag something to read on the journey: the book that May had given to her, William Morris's verse translation of some story from an old Icelandic saga.

The compartment she entered was barely half full. To her relief, nobody else came aboard at Swindon. The sprinkle of passengers had the wearily resigned appearance of people already subjected to quite enough jolting and lurching on their way here from Bath or some intermediate point of embarkation but conscious that most of their journey to London still lay ahead. She sat facing a pale timid-looking woman of about her own age and size, dowdily dressed, who gave a diffident little nod of greeting but then withdrew into herself like a timorous snail. A whistle blew, doors were closed, and gradually the train creaked into motion.

With her handkerchief pressed to her mouth, and making little throat-clearing noises from time to time, the young woman opposite gazed out at the passing countryside until dusk leached the last light from the day and nothing more could be seen through the grimy window. Then she folded her hands and looked down at them for a long while. Perhaps she was praying?

When Lucy spoke to her she started. 'Beg your pardon, Ma'am,' she said, wheezing. 'Not sure what you said. I was…I was in a sort of dream. I've never been this far away from my birthplace before.' There was an unmistakable Bristol burr in her voice, with a trilling of the 'r' sound.

Lucy gave her a smile of reassurance. 'I just asked whether you're travelling right through to London.'

'Oh. Yes. And then a long way further,' she said. 'For my health.' She gave an indicative cough.

They introduced themselves. The sickly woman's name was Isabella Trent.

Paddington

to

Fremantle

1889

SIXTEEN

*T*HERE WAS SOMETHING FORLORN IN ISABELLA'S MANNER, and it piqued Lucy's curiosity. As they were to be together for several hours, putting casual questions would do more than pass the time; it would help to subdue Lucy's misgivings about her own situation and drive from her mind the horror of what she had left behind in Swindon.

So she drew her travel companion into conversation and coaxed information from her. First journey away from home and family, was it? Intending to travel far beyond London? Despite being troubled, apparently, by health problems?

Isabella said that she grew up in Bristol but no longer had any family members living there. 'Or anywhere else, far as I know,' she added wistfully. 'Quite alone in the world now, see.' It was the recent death of her mother that prompted her to leave home in search of work and a change of climate. Having suffered for some while from a lung complaint that was also weakening her heart, she had decided on her doctor's advice to emigrate to Australia in the hope that its warm weather would bring better health. A friend from her local church had put her in contact with the United British Women's Emigration Association, which was, she had been assured, a highly respectable Christian organisation.

Bit by bit, as the miles went clacketing by, Isabella told Lucy what she knew about how the scheme worked. Being short of breath, she dispensed the details slowly. The head of the Association, Mrs Ellen Joyce, personally selected parties of single women twice a year to be sponsored for voyages to certain British colonies in faraway lands, Australia or New Zealand or Canada, with a view to employment in domestic service. The vicar of Isabella's parish had helped her compose a letter of application and supplied a testimonial to accompany it. A couple of months later, Mrs Joyce travelled to Bristol from her home in Winchester to interview Isabella.

'I felt anxious before we met,' she said, 'not knowing what to expect.' Lucy could hear a faint sussuration in Isabella's chest as she spoke. 'And then Mrs Joyce's manner was quite stern, though underneath it she seemed kindly enough. Anyhow, she must have been satisfied.' A letter of acceptance followed, with a clothing list and other practical instructions. She would be the only person from Bristol in a group of about 50 young women travelling to a port called Fremantle in the colony of Western Australia. 'So here I goes. Nervous, I don't mind telling you. Heart in my mouth.' And phlegm in your lungs, poor girl, thought Lucy. Not auspicious for a long sea voyage.

The arrangement made by letter, Isabella explained drowsily, was that she should meet her party at Blackwall Pier on the afternoon of the 16th of August.

'Tomorrow, then!' said Lucy. 'So what will you do tonight, after our train reaches Paddington Station? Where will you stay?'

'I hope to find a hotel – one that won't cost more than I can afford, mind. I don't know London at all, but I'm told there's a goodly number of places with cheap rooms.'

'Hmm. By the time we arrive it will be quite late. Hansom cabs are expensive and you won't want to be trudging around those grimy gas-lit streets in search of accommodation.' Lucy paused before adding, 'But I have an idea.'

She invited Isabella to share a room with her at Paddington Station's Great Western Royal Hotel – so conveniently situated, just a short walk from the platform where they would arrive, and such a huge building that there would surely be a two-bed room available for them. No cost to Isabella, certainly not: Lucy insisted on covering it in full. She waved away Isabella's profuse expressions of gratitude. 'It will be a pleasure to help you, my dear. Now let's try to get some rest.'

Cold draughts had crept into their compartment, and there were no foot-warmers in second class. Lucy tucked her coat more tightly around her legs. Isabella, looking weary and whey-faced, wrapped herself in a thin blanket from her travelling case, coughed up mucus into her handkerchief, and then sank into sleep.

In Lucy's mind, welling grief kept fatigue at bay. She could not rid her mind of a flux of scenes from that afternoon: Julius swaying at the front door of the villa, sitting dispiritedly in her drawing room, trying to offer comfort after her anguished outburst, wrestling with Gerard, toppling back senseless, lying inert on the floor. But then something else pushed those stark, terrible images aside: a gush of desperation as she tried to think what she must do next.

She was acutely conscious of being suspended in a restless limbo: she had no planned course of action beyond seeking

May's advice, no sense of any ultimate goal ahead and no place behind her to which she could return. Go back to Swindon? Unimaginable. The town itself was so small and dull, with nothing more to offer than an occasional amateur concert in the Drill Hall, a modest lending library in the Mechanics Institute, and an unremarkable cluster of shops. Besides, after the harrowing things that had happened she couldn't tolerate the thought of living any longer under the same roof with Gerard. Nor, though she sorely missed May's company, could she envisage taking up employment again at Merton Abbey; it seemed unthinkable now to resume her position there as if her whole life hadn't changed utterly. Making her way back to Staffordshire was also quite out of the question: there would be nothing for her in Leek. Even Mrs Wardle's Embroidery Society would hardly be congenial after all this time. Since its great national success in producing an admired replica of the Bayeux Tapestry it had reportedly confined its attention to altar cloths and ecclesiastical vestments – not the kind of work that could hold much interest for Lucy these days.

Adrift in a haze of regretful yearning, she wished she could just turn into someone else, a new person altogether, and felt almost envious of Isabella, who had the prospect of reshaping herself in an entirely new place.

As the train steamed at last into Paddington Station, Lucy shook Isabella awake. Soon an immoderately merry young porter took charge of their luggage and led the way to the Great Western Royal Hotel at the head of the station. Although its imposing bulk and extravagant ornamentation were not new to Lucy, she looked up now at the facade with the same wonder she had felt on first seeing it: tall solid towers at either end, a classical pediment echoed by smaller triangular shapes above the many windows, an elaborately allegorical sculpture over the front doorway – in every feature it declared itself to be a grand temple to the spirit of commerce. Isabella appeared utterly awestruck, standing at the entrance wide-eyed and open-mouthed and then, as she moved hesitantly behind Lucy into the vestibule, gasping with astonishment at a pair of large electrical clocks.

Before long they were in their room, unlacing boots, unbuttoning garments, unpacking nightgowns, and yawning as they talked.

'So *big*, this bedroom!' exclaimed Isabella. 'I do hope it won't stop me getting off to sleep, the size of it. And goodness me! What you must be paying – the expense don't bear thinking about!'

'Then don't think about it,' said Lucy breezily. 'I'm not lacking money, so providing us both with a night's shelter and rest is a simple matter.'

They settled into their comfortable beds and talked on for a while. Isabella said the instructions she had been given for the following day were clear enough: she would find her way to Fenchurch Street station, and take a train to Blackwall Pier, where her party was to gather in the Emigrant Depot. But she confessed to feeling apprehensive about what lay ahead. Although Mrs Joyce had assured her that their shipboard matron, Miss Monk, was 'a good-hearted friendly soul,' the thought of getting quickly acquainted with a large group of fellow emigrants from all over the country was unnerving. 'I'm a bit shy, see?' And she worried, too, about having to cope with a long sea voyage. 'I may find it quite an ordeal, not being the hardy sort. Right now, just thinking on it all, there's such a thumping in my chest. Makes me ever so breathless.'

Listening to the whistle in Isabella's throat and imagining the palpitations, Lucy talked to her in a calm and comforting tone, until at length the wheeziness seemed to diminish. Then Lucy let herself drift toward sleep.

She woke slowly as morning light began to leak in at the edges of the curtains and a medley of noises rose up from street and railway. There was no movement from Isabella's bed, so Lucy opened their door quietly and walked along the corridor to the water closet. When she returned she tipped a jug of water into the washstand and sponged her face and arms. Isabella remained motionless and silent. Puzzled at being unable to hear the girl's breath rattling and hissing as it had done the night before, Lucy went over and touched her gently on the forehead. The waxen flesh was deathly cold. Alarmed, Lucy cried out, tapped Isabella's shoulder. Shook it hard. No response. No life in her.

Recoiling panic-stricken from the corpse, Lucy sat down limply, face in her hands, assailed by nausea and a welter of questions. What did this sudden death require her to do? Should she ask the hotel manager to summon a doctor? The police? As Isabella had no relatives, who else ought to be notified, and how? What of the emigration party that was expecting her to join them that afternoon? The matron would need to be told – what was her name?

Her nerves felt like a whirl of flustered pigeons, and she needed to steady them. Remembering the bottle that she had wrapped in a petticoat, she took it from her Gladstone bag and quickly poured herself a large glass. The ruby colour of the sloe gin brought to mind for a moment the bright coils of silk piled on a trestle one sunlit afternoon at the Merton Abbey works. How long ago it now seemed, that idyll: an irretrievably distant haven of contentment. She brushed it aside.

As if aroused by the tang of the gin, a sudden idea came to her, strange and heady. Apart from Lucy, nobody in London knew who this dead woman was, nobody at all. Her name would be on the shipboard matron's list of emigrants, but it was possible for another person to step forward at Blackwall Pier as 'Isabella' without raising any suspicion. Lucy herself could do this – and it might be the solution to her quandary. Hadn't she felt envious of Isabella's prospects? Hadn't she longed to turn into someone else? Here then, fortuitously, was the perfect opportunity: she could become Isabella, present herself as one of the chosen group members, travel to the far side of the world, leave her losses and sorrows behind, and start a new life.

The choice was so intoxicating that it made her hands tremble. She should try to moderate her impetuosity, she told herself, considering carefully the practical aspects of such an audacious impersonation. It would mean getting away from the hotel as soon as possible while silently abandoning Isabella's body here. But first, of course, she would need to dress in the clothes that Isabella had worn yesterday. Her own bag she must leave in the room, taking only a little money and a few anonymous personal items from it. Isabella's luggage would now be hers. Looking through it, she found the all-important sponsorship papers from the United British Women's Emigration Association and the letter from Mrs Joyce with its attached information. On the list of required clothing, Isabella had put a tick beside each item, and Lucy could see them all neatly folded there: half a dozen chemises, two flannel petticoats, half a dozen pairs of stockings, two pairs of boots, two plain thick gowns. With these modest possessions she would equip herself for the transformation she had hastily begun to anticipate. Did she have the gumption to follow it all through? Yes. She felt resolute. She would do it.

Within a few minutes she was on her way downstairs, leaving Isabella's heavy bag, which she must now regard as her own, outside the door to their room. Finding a porter, she sent him up to fetch it, tipping him handsomely and mentioning that her friend, having been indisposed, was still fast asleep and shouldn't be disturbed earlier than necessary. She then settled payment for the room and immediately took a hansom cab to Fenchurch Street station. Although there was no hurry to arrive there, she could spend a few hours in its waiting room before the short rail journey to Blackwall Pier. Meanwhile, it was urgent to get away from the Paddington hotel.

She flinched at the thought of Isabella's forsaken body. It was hard-hearted of her to have left the poor waif behind so unceremoniously, looking as spiritless as one of Madame Tussaud's effigies. Even more shocking was the reckless boldness of her flight: she was on the point of renouncing all that had ever been personally significant. Places where her life had taken shape or decisively changed direction: Leek, London, Swindon. Places known more briefly, but indelibly imprinted on her soul: Ticehurst House asylum with its sad inmates, the farm at Stratton St Margaret where that terrifying bull went on the rampage, the Cheddleton Mills and the unforgotten riverside episode there. And not only places; she was also turning her back on experiences that had brought her such pleasure or distress: the artistry she had found in fine needlework, the deep friendship with May, the intellectual stimulus of the Arts and Crafts circle and the Socialist League, the rivalrous love of two men, one now dead and the other his hapless killer...

Her husband the killer: what did she now feel about Gerard? Guilt, yes, at having provoked him by her cruelly frank words, so that when he later thought Julius was assaulting her he reacted with vengeful passion. Guilt, too, at having deserted him, which meant he would have to face alone the consequences of that death – yet it was she, in effect, who had caused it, though he had struck the blow. And it occurred to her that, by absconding like this after a violent incident in her home, she was not only treating Gerard unjustly but probably also breaking the law. While she was not an accomplice or an accessory, surely as a sole witness she had a legal obligation to stay? Be that as it may, what tugged at her conscience was her personal disloyalty. She was leaving Gerard comfortless, this earnest and decent man who undoubtedly loved her, whose name she had taken, whose bed she had shared, and whose child she had been carrying until the farm accident.

And what of Julius, the one who had stirred her emotions more deeply than Gerard for all his worthiness ever could, and who had made her flesh sing despite the fact that their bodies had never joined except in the formal gestures of dance? Only yesterday he had been appealing to her, speaking with a directness that brought her to furious tears, and now his voice with its rich timbre had fallen permanently silent. There had hardly been time yet to accept the fact of his death, much less to begin to mourn a life extinguished in such a pointless manner. But already, before yesterday's dreadful incident, she had lost him several times over, and it was hard to untangle the causal threads in that recurrent pattern. Part of it was her perverse habit of slighting him; she was still unsure why she had behaved so wilfully. But he also bore responsibility, did he not, for giving priority to his military career, withdrawing from her into a wordless distance and rupturing whatever trust they once had in each other? For reasons that would remain opaque to her, those years in India and Burma had sapped something vital in his character.

Much of her past had become so painful that she could never turn back now. By leaving the hotel in the guise of someone else, she had committed herself impulsively and irrevocably to exile in Western Australia, a place she could barely yet envisage. She knew even less about her destination than about the exotic oriental countries that Kendrick's letters had sketched in such a cursory way. Lucy clasped her gloved hands as if in prayer.

A day later, just as she began to tell herself with a sense of relief that the deception had been successful, something unforeseen would make it appear inevitable that she was about to be exposed as an imposter.

SEVENTEEN

*T*HOUGH UNPLEASANT, THE RAIL JOURNEY FROM Fenchurch Street to Blackwall Pier was brief enough to be tolerable. Like most of the passengers she travelled third-class, and in her case it was a prudent choice. As there might well be other young women on their way to join the same group, she had no wish to be a noticeable exception to what they would naturally assume: that frugality was a basic principle for all sponsored emigrant women. Her carriage, crowded and dirty, had the repugnant odour of unwashed bodies. She smiled to herself wryly, remembering Morris's description of the urban railway system as 'a vapour-bath of hurried and discontented humanity.'

Between Fenchurch Street and Blackwall Pier the train passed through several shabby stations, but when she emerged from the terminus and stepped onto a pebbly promenade she found herself beside a large bend in the river with extensive views in both directions. A few large ships rode at anchor out there on the water, surrounded by a flock of red-sailed barges, while along the wharfside there was all the bustle of loading, unloading, carting and stacking – with other activities whose purpose seemed inscrutable.

Odd pieces of heavy masonry lay scattered around the pier, the residue of some forgotten project. Leaning indolently against one large block was a young man with a wild thatch of yellow hair, whom she asked for directions to the Emigrant Depot. He jabbed the air with his clay pipe, pointing towards a large building not far away. 'See where them bow windows are stickin out? That's it.'

Dragging her cumbersome bag, she made her way slowly to the indicated place and went through its large entrance doorway. At one side of the vestibule a plump middle-aged woman sat behind an incongruously small table on which a handwritten sign was propped: *United British Women's Emigration Association. Register here.* Their eyes met.

'Emigrating to Western Australia, yes? Over here then, please. Good afternoon. Name?'

'Isabella Trent.' The lie was easy; the die was cast.

The woman introduced herself as 'Miss Mary Monk, your shipboard matron,' welcomed 'Isabella' with a few benign words and a warm smile, and put a tick beside her name on a list.

'Now, Miss Trent,' she went on briskly, 'here's what you're to do next. Take that travelling bag of yours to the dormitory upstairs – turn right at the top, along to the far end of the passage – and leave it on whichever bed you choose, provided it doesn't already have someone else's bag on it. And then...' (Miss Monk consulted her pocket watch) 'in just over an hour, five o'clock sharp, you must be in the dining room at the opposite end of the same upstairs corridor. That's where all members of our party will gather. After our meal I'll have some information to impart to everyone. Meanwhile you'll find some of your fellow emigrants in the dormitory or outside the dining room, so you'll be able to make yourselves known to each other.'

Entering the dormitory, short of breath from the effort of lugging her heavy bag up the staircase and along the passage, she saw more than a dozen women perched on their chosen beds. All were dressed in standard black and white, as she was. Our uniform of sober humility, whispered her inner voice. Not one of them wore anything that displayed even the smallest splash of colour. She greeted the group collectively and there was a slow ripple of murmured responses. The mood seemed subdued. If there is any excitement among them, she thought, apprehensive feelings are keeping it in check. Probably nobody in our party has much idea of what the long sea voyage will be like, or what awaits us at our distant destination.

She reminded herself that she must maintain the deferential manner of an aspiring domestic servant. Yet surely it would be unnecessary to disguise her usual way of speaking, except that she should care to avoid mention of anything that might proclaim her affinity with a comfortable social class. Nobody here knew where the real Isabella had lived, so there was no risk in letting the verbal traces of her own Staffordshire origin come through naturally. If it transpired that Isabella was shown in Miss Monk's notes as coming from Bristol, a plausible story would be that she had recently moved there from Leek.

They sat awkwardly around the dormitory like figures in an improvised tableau. Most were silent; a few made desultory conversation. A voice from the corner of the room called out chirpily, 'Look at us, twiddling our thumbs. A bevy of ladies in waiting, ain't we!' Deeming this the acme of wittiness, a snaggle-toothed girl on the bed next to Isabella's responded with whinnying mirth, and then sighed appreciatively 'Dear me, oh dear me' as a prelude to telling Isabella her name was Penny Priddle. Isabella did her best to engage this new interlocutor in small talk, but found no common ground. Time crawled until someone remarked that the meal was nearly due to be served. They walked together to the other end of the corridor.

Looking around the balconied dining room, Isabella could imagine that it would have been more grandly furnished in the building's heyday. Half a dozen plain deal tables were now spaced evenly along the length of the room, each with an assortment of motley chairs. Penny Priddle attached herself to Isabella, and they took the last couple of places at one of the tables. Food soon arrived: grey roast beef and a watery mash of potatoes. Though none of them ate with gusto, little was left on their plates after ten minutes of steady chewing. 'Well, I didn't much like the look of it,' declared Penny Priddle to her table companions, 'but it's a fair bellyful, innit?' Dollops of rice pudding followed, and then Miss Monk addressed the group.

She told them that this Emigrant Depot had once been the Brunswick Hotel, famous for its whitebait delicacies. Those glory days were past, but it was an entirely convenient place for pausing before 'our big adventure.' The group would be spending five nights there. This interval was necessary, she explained, because some important preliminary matters had to be dealt with before they could embark. For one thing, each person would undergo a medical examination to ensure that they were all fit for sea travel and free of any ailments that might make them unsuitable for employment in the colony of Western Australia. Sleeping arrangements in the Depot would prepare them for the cramped conditions on board, and they would also become accustomed during this pre-departure period to undertaking various chores within their mess. There were to be six messes, each of eight women.

'Your particular mess is the group in which you are now sitting,' Miss Monk said. 'So look around your table: these are the people you will share certain duties with until our ship arrives in Fremantle. Your mess will eat together, draw rations, cook, clean and so forth, in accordance with timetables and rules to be issued to you within the next day or two.'

Miss Monk made some amiable concluding remarks and was about to resume her seat when, apparently as an afterthought, she announced something that threw Isabella into trepidation.

'By the way,' she told them, 'you can expect a special visitor tomorrow evening. Mrs Ellen Joyce, head of the Association that arranges and subsidises your emigration, usually comes here just before each party sets forth. She likes to dispense some words of encouragement and advice. Most of you have met her, of course, because she personally interviews as many applicants as possible during the selection process. I'm sure you'll show respect when you see her again tomorrow. And gratitude, of course.'

That night Isabella found sleep elusive, not only because the narrow bed was so rigid but also because of her worries about Mrs Joyce's visit and the unmasking that would surely follow. She could envisage no way to avoid having her deception exposed. Mrs Joyce would see immediately that she was not the real Isabella. This would involve public shame, and no doubt bring her to the attention of police, who would eventually connect her to the pair of recent deaths, the one in her New Swindon house and the one in the hotel room she had shared at Paddington Station. At first she thought of remaining in bed for the day, feigning acute sickness; but she soon recognised that this was not feasible, as it would put in jeopardy the clean bill of health needed for emigration. No other stratagem occurred to her. She was certain to be denounced as criminally deceitful. Meanwhile the restless night dragged on.

Enervated by fatigue and dread, she took no part in table talk the next morning and could hardly summon the energy to wash down her lumpy porridge with a mug of tea. The ensuing hours were largely taken up with instruction and practice in the routines of mess duty, and then with a stern talk by Miss Monk about the need for 'proper conduct' during the voyage: there must, above all, be no conversation with male passengers or crew, no immodest behaviour of any kind, and no straying outside the designated precinct to which the emigrant party would be strictly confined except, on occasion, when allowed by the matron's explicit consent.

So preoccupied was Isabella with her apprehensions about being confronted imminently by Mrs Joyce that she had not listened with full attention to Miss Monk's words, and almost missed the fact that a miraculous reprieve had occurred. Turning to Priddle, she whispered, 'What did she just say? Something about Mrs Joyce?'

'The lady won't be paying us a visit after all. Been took real sick.'

Isabella had to stop herself from clapping her hands and shouting with sheer relief. The danger of discovery had passed – at least for the time being.

Over the next couple of days she formed clear impressions of the women in her mess and did her best to hide what she thought, not wanting to seem standoffish. She couldn't help wishing there were some livelier souls among them. The truth was that they appeared to be a dull lot. Their colourless clothing had its counterpart in their monotonous conversation. It would be unfair, she told herself, to blame them for that; most of them presumably had only an elementary education and no opportunity to talk with anyone from outside their family, neighbourhood and social group.

She felt a small jolt at the thought that the high-minded socialism of Morris and his circle, which she had found so appealing, stemmed from a rose-coloured view of the artisan class and paid little attention to the drab circumstances of the servant class. The Socialist League, she now recognised, had been earnest in pursuing broad ideals of justice and equality without looking closely at the everyday constraints that narrowed the attitudes of working people such as these women around her.

Keenly aware that she should suppress her tendency to withdraw and hold herself at a distance from others, Isabella tried to see each of her seven messmates as a distinct individual with whom she could forge a particular relationship. As a first step she quickly memorised their names, mentally linking them one by one with some obvious mannerism, feature or attribute.

Meg Dyce, a stolid and diligent woman, reminded her of Perkins, her aunt's faithful retainer, and no doubt had a heart of gold, as Perkins did, though that wasn't enough to make her a particularly congenial companion. There was Penny Priddle, good-natured in a vacuous way, who attached herself unshakably to Isabella. The meek cousins, Emily and Constance Miller, were both so short and slender that they made her think of spindles. Rhoda Gadsden wore a fixed smile, as if determined to radiate cheer whatever hardships might befall her. Hope Smollett kept her pale head lowered and seldom uttered a word. Ruth Fitch, the hardest to befriend, had a surly lip-curling demeanour, and seemed bent on denying the spirit of her given name, being pitilessly truculent towards others.

With luck, thought Isabella, a few of them might later reveal more interesting qualities than were visible on the surface. Meanwhile, all she could do was to conceal – or better, attempt to overcome – her lack of enthusiasm for their company, making an effort to be pleasant to them all.

On the morning of their scheduled departure she woke early. Nobody else was stirring. There would be mess duties before breakfast and bags to pack afterwards, but she wanted now to have a few minutes to herself – time to contemplate briefly the disconcerting fact that this would be her last day in England for a very long while if not forever. She went quietly down the stairs and peered through one of large bow windows at the river mist, not yet beginning to lift. The first touch of sun tickled its wispy fringes. This part of the Docks would soon shake itself into another day's activity, reawakened to its linkage with the ends of the earth. It was, she knew, a place where the comings and goings of worldwide commerce and industry converged and countless exchanges occurred. Merchandise was arriving regularly from the farthest reaches of the empire – rice and jute, wool and wheat, seed and frozen meat; while among the cargo shipped off to some of those same distant places there were often batches of emigrants. As if to confess that no such transaction was ethically fragrant, the afternoon's easterly wind would bring a strong odour from guano works further down the river.

She made her way back towards the dormitory, conscious that there was still some doubt as to whether their embarkation, planned for that day, would be delayed after all. Information from Miss Monk combined with mess gossip had spread the word that they might not get away before the impending strike of many thousands of dock labourers put a stop to all river traffic and the loading of vessels. For the last week there had been unrest on the wharves and processions in the nearby streets, with crowds of men milling around and chanting demands that were audible through the walls of the Emigrant Depot: 'Dockers' tanner! Dockers' tanner! Sixpence an hour, that's all we ask!' Meg Dyce expressed sympathy with the workers' cause; the Miller cousins fretted, saying anxiously that they didn't know where all this agitation might end up; Penny Priddle dismissed the matter with a shrug, confident that they needn't give it a moment's thought once they sailed off to their new lives in a colony that would surely be free of England's wretched poverty.

To their surprise the morning passed without incident. Evidently the expected strike had not yet happened, and so just before midday they went aboard a long barge, which took them with all their boxes and bags to the screw steamer that was to be their floating home for many weeks, the SS *Nairnshire*. It awaited them at Gravesend, an hour and a half downriver with the tide.

After anchoring overnight near the river mouth, their ship moved out into the Channel with favourable winds. They were all permitted to stroll around the afterdeck for an hour and watch the receding shoreline. Standing at the taffrail, she bade a silent final goodbye to her discarded self as its ghost floated towards land like the gradually dissolving foam of the ship's wake. Then she turned away from it. She must shun regret. She must relinquish every lingering particle of what belonged to the Lucy phase of her existence. She must learn to inhabit this entirely different person, this Isabella, without a backward glance.

EIGHTEEN

NEVER HAVING SEEN ANYTHING LIKE THE *NAIRNSHIRE* before, nobody in the emigrant party had imagined that their ship would be so huge or so handsomely fitted out. For the first week at sea they could talk of little else, marvelling that it was over a hundred yards long, that its steam engines were said to be powerful enough to drive the vessel forward at a steady speed in all weathers, that it was equipped with refrigeration chambers reportedly capable of transporting an immense quantity of frozen meat from New Zealand back to England, and that its electrical system lit up the aft saloon at night with astonishing splendour – or so Miss Monk told them; they had no access to that sanctum themselves.

Their own steerage quarters were far less commodious. As assisted emigrants they could hardly expect much elbow-room, let alone anything approaching luxury. Irksome though the conditions were to Isabella, she made no comment on them to the other women. They too might be finding some of the shipboard restrictions difficult, but unlike her they would not have been accustomed to a life of ease. Here they all slept in narrow berths that lined the walls below the main deck, surrounded by unpleasant smells. Any clothes and supplies required during the voyage had to be kept in canvas bags under the beds while their other possessions were packed into trunks and stored in the hold. The only substantial piece of furniture in their nether part of the ship was a long dining table, sturdy though inelegant. They had heard that the spacious saloon above them was richly decorated with oak, mahogany and other fine woods, but in steerage everything looked plain and unvarnished.

Isabella soon found that the shape of every day was strictly determined. Chores took up several morning hours, varying somewhat according to the roster but generally following a simple routine. Within each mess they had their appointed tasks: there were always floors to be scrubbed, dishes to be washed, sleeping areas to be cleaned, clothes and bedding to be shaken out and tidied. When their mess also took its turn to draw rations and prepare food for the whole party, they needed to carry water, fetch the allocations of preserved meat and bottled porter, and serve the carefully meted quantities of oatmeal porridge, rice pudding, pea soup, potatoes or whatever else the ship's kitchen had provided for that day's meals.

This regimen of collective duties required Isabella to interact closely with her messmates, but she was wary of getting drawn into unnecessary talk. Any little lapse on her part – a seemingly innocuous comment, a slightly inconsistent detail – could lay bare the falseness of her identity. Yet while preferring to keep to herself she remained well aware that aloofness was unwise, and scarcely possible most of the time anyhow. Afternoons did offer some respite, usually allowing her to read in a quiet corner rather than join in the deck games. But the thing that could not be avoided was for her the most troublesome activity of all:

a series of compulsory lessons in basic needlework skills. She had to pretend she knew almost as little as most of the other women, and listen with a show of attentiveness while Matron Monk revealed the arcane mysteries of cutting cloth, sewing, and making blouses for themselves. There was regular instruction in a few different kinds of stitching. Nearly all of them could already darn a hole with simple cross-woven running stitches, but anything more elaborate had to be ploddingly demonstrated and assiduously practised. Isabella gritted her teeth as she went through the tedium of this simulated apprenticeship.

As single women whose sound moral character would be their chief claim to employability in the colony, they were segregated and kept under close watch by the Matron. Talking with male passengers or crew was expressly forbidden. For Isabella, this was no great privation; men had brought her scant happiness in the past, and she wanted to keep her distance from them.

Evenings were the most difficult time. Except for 'special events' such the insipid concerts occasionally staged by saloon passengers, the Matron would order her group to stay below deck after dark, and be in their berths by nine o'clock. Those who were moderately literate would often fill in the hours before sleep by writing letters or diaries, but the murky light and cramped conditions made it awkward to put pen to paper, even when the ship was not rolling. Isabella had considered writing to May Morris, who by now would probably have heard of her disappearance and Kendrick's death – but decided against it. What would be the point? How would she be able to explain, even to such a sympathetic friend, her impulse to flee from the life she had lived for 27 years? The circumstances that made her become a fugitive? What reasons might she give for choosing exile in this way, concealing – indeed repudiating – what had previously been her true self? If she tried to describe in a letter the effort she was now making to blend into the company of these uncongenial fellow-emigrants, or the prospect of working as a domestic servant in an arid outpost of empire, what sense could May make of it? She herself hardly understood what she had done.

So in the evenings, while some wrote and others sang or played card games like Beggar My Neighbour, Isabella lay in her berth and began to hold silent imaginary conversations with people from her abandoned 'Lucy world,' as she now thought of it. The resolution, made at the point of leaving England's shores, to forget that world completely had been futile. She managed to push her past down out of sight during the daylight hours, but with darkness it rose again into her mind, peopled with ghosts who spoke to her and listened to her thoughts. Julius Kendrick and Gerard Barton. The Morris family. The Wardles. Aunt Barbara. Her father.

Conflict within their emigrant party first emerged soon after the *Nairnshire* encountered rough weather in the Bay of Biscay. Unremitting gales and high seas kept them all below deck for days. The simplest things turned into tests of patience, and mealtimes became especially difficult as plates and cutlery slid off the table and clattered across the tilting floor. For those on mess duty, fetching provisions was now hazardous because heavy boxes and barrels swung erratically around the storage area. Hour after hour most of the women lay on their bunks, groaning and sweating. A stink of vomit and slopping chamber pots filled the air. On the second stormy day the Miller cousins raised their quavering voices in a dirge:

Eternal Father, strong to save,
Whose arm hath bound the restless wave,
Who bidd'st the mighty ocean deep
Its own appointed limits keep;
Oh, hear us when we cry to Thee,
For those in peril on the sea!

'Aarh, I wish you'd shuddup!' shouted Ruth Fitch. 'You're like a pair of yowling alley cats.' Seemingly impervious to seasickness, she had been steadily quaffing porter – not only her own bottle but those allocated to Rhoda Gadsden and Hope Smollett as well. They were both teetotallers, and she insisted that they should pass their share on to her. The extra drinking made her more obstreperous than usual. Even before embarkation she had shown herself to be hostile to everyone, as if holding a grudge against the world in general, and during the voyage her malice became implacable, her vituperation unrelenting. Behind her back Meg Dyce murmured a verdict: 'Ruth Fitch? Ruthless Bitch!' – and others gleefully repeated this epithet in whispers. Miss Monk twice took Fitch aside and urged her not to pick quarrels, but she took no notice.

And now, made bellicose by drink, she had the inoffensive Miller girls in her sights. When she yelled at them they stopped singing, but Fitch was not going to let it rest there. 'Everyone hates them dreary hymns of yourn!' she declared in her loud rasping voice. 'No wonder most folk is feeling bilious.'

Isabella couldn't stop herself from remonstrating. 'Leave those poor girls alone,' she said. 'Their singing does no harm to anybody, and it's a solace to some. You should keep your bad temper to yourself.'

Fitch turned slowly towards her and glared with a smouldering malevolence. 'Hark now at Madam High-and-Mighty!' she spat out. 'Who are you to tell me what to do? Think your pretty face and lofty talk makes you better'n the rest of us, dontcha? So whatcha doing here among a pack of lowly servants, eh?'

Isabella looked away, biting her tongue. Stupid to have spoken up like that in a tone of cold rebuke. And not just stupid, but arrogant too: for while Fitch was openly ruthless, hadn't Isabella herself been secretly ruthless in leaving Gerard to his fate and abandoning the body of the girl whose name she stole? Did her dislike of Fitch stem partly from half-recognising something it would be uncomfortable to admit: that Fitch's behaviour expressed in caricature a nasty streak in her own character? In any case, Isabella thought, she must keep her judgments to herself. Fitch could be a dangerous enemy, perhaps a half-deranged one, but shrewd. They would be tripping over one another for several more weeks at sea, and then they might cross paths again after arrival in the colony. Best to be on her guard.

At the time of departure each female emigrant had been supplied with a single item of reading matter. Mrs Joyce's cautionary pamphlet *Letter to Girls on Leaving England* was full of warnings about perilous temptations on board and afterwards. It inveighed against dancing, staying late on deck, chattering with men, spending wages on clothes, and various other bad habits. Isabella skimmed through it quickly, amused at its anxious concern with averting improper conduct. The pamphlet was not worth a second glance, but she wished she had more things to read. In the haste of leaving Swindon she had brought with her only one printed item: the book that May had given her, William Morris's long poem *The Lovers of Gudrun*. She would have to absorb it unhurriedly. Taking it one morning from the bag at the end of her berth, she began to read.

It seized her attention at once, as if a powerful hand had stretched out from the page and gripped her by the shoulder.

The Lovers of Gudrun took the form of an extensive narrative poem, she could see that at a glance; but placed separately before the first line of verse was a single prose sentence summarising what would follow – and it spoke to her with a directness that made her gasp. 'This story shows how two friends loved a fair woman,' said the synopsis, 'and how he who loved her best had her to wife, though she loved him little or not at all, and how one of these friends gave shame to and received death of the other...' In essence, it was *her* tale! Breathing fast, she read on feverishly. Couched in archaic phrasing, the rhyming couplets transported her to the saga-shaped world of medieval Iceland – a weird and distant world, yet one in which an uncannily familiar situation was unfolding as she turned the pages. Many of the descriptive details and narrative turns had no parallel in her own experience, but she disregarded them and fastened upon the story's fateful core with a sense of shocked recognition. She saw a tragedy unfolding inexorably with all the stealth of what the poem called 'slow-foot time.' Although Kiartan and his foster brother Bodli grew up in cheerful friendship on their family's farmstead, even in their early days a local seer could glimpse portents of 'inter-woven miseries' awaiting them. By the time that Kiartan, having developed into a seemingly flawless warrior, fell in love with the beautiful Gudrun, whose golden tresses shone 'finer than silk,' it was clear that future trouble hovered over them 'as on unheard wings / The kestrel hangs above the mouse.'

Having to put the book aside at that point and report for mess duties, Isabella herself felt suspended in mid-air like the kestrel, but also exposed to danger like the mouse. The tension pervading the story spilled over into her own state of mind, and she felt acutely frustrated at being unable to resume her reading until some hours later. This became the pattern for several days. She wanted to press forward with more of the poem, brushing aside any episodes that deviated from the central chain of events to which her own life story seemed to correspond – but Morris's mannered, periphrastic style of writing often slowed her down with puzzling turns of phrase or with paradoxical expressions that made her linger, such as 'love slaying love, and ruinous victory.' Besides, there were no secluded nooks where she could read on without interruptions, and the story was so *long* – spun out like filamentary yarn over several thousand lines of verse.

So she went back to it eagerly as often as she could, with an intensity that had become obsessive. She read, she looked up from the page, she read again, and the characters drawn by Morris from Icelandic literature merged into the person she had been and the men who had loved her.

When Kiartan and Bodli went overseas to fight for the Norwegian king, and Kiartan stayed away while Bodli returned to woo Gudrun, Isabella re-entered her Lucy world and relived what she had suffered in the absence of Kendrick and the presence of Barton. When Kiartan was slain she felt herself returning to all the horror of that last day in Swindon, and wept at the passage that depicted 'Bodli standing over Kiartan's head, / His friend, his foster-brother, and his bane.' When she reached the story's end, closing in on the remorseful words of an aged and lonely Gudrun, she whispered them to herself, over and over, and then turned back to the opening pages and started to read the whole book again.

Most nights now she would lie awake for hours on end as the thrum of engines and the rhythm of Morris's poetry resounded together in her head. She imagined that she could hear the author's voice, so well known to her, reciting his lines, and the thought came that the story's doomed triad of lovers had a further real-life counterpart, not only matching in such a painfully exact way her own relationships with Julius and Gerard and theirs with each other but also reflecting the three-cornered knot of passion binding Morris so tightly to his wife Jane and to her lover and his close friend, Rossetti.

As these connections multiplied in her mind she began to feel ill, swollen with distress, and wondered whether she might be going mad. *The Lovers of Gudrun* was agitating all the painful things she had wanted to forget. There were renewed stirrings of guilt, too – guilt at usurping the identity of the real Isabella and abandoning her nameless corpse in the hotel, guilt at letting Gerard face the police alone, guilt at leaving Julius lying dead on the floor. There was an upsurge of regret for so much that she had left behind. And there was the old confusion of feelings about that day with her father on Ffiney Mede near the Cheddleton Mills.

Guildford
and
Fremantle
1890-97

NINETEEN

WHEN ISABELLA FIRST SAW THE HOUSE WHERE THE course of her life would take another violent turn just months later, it seemed an entirely innocuous place.

She paused for breath at the street gate. Walking here from the Guildford railway station had taken only a few minutes, but the weather was hot and her bag heavy. Though lighter clothing would have been more comfortable, Miss Monk's strict advice was that decorum allowed no choice about what to wear for such occasions. Taking out a handkerchief, she wiped her face. Two barefoot children playing under a large mottle-bark tree nearby had confirmed with nods that this was the Oram house.

She straightened her bonnet and stood looking. While making her way along Ethel Street she had seen several single-storey cottages like this one, each sitting squarely within its own separate little domestic precinct, framed by a paling fence and bisected by a path running straight from street to door. All these dwellings displayed similar features. There was a newly built freshness in their red brickwork, an attractive breadth in their shady verandahs, and a pleasant symmetry in the way their sash windows flanked a centrally positioned front door with slim panes of coloured glass on either side of door and windows. But this house in front of her was larger than the others, and its neat garden, brightly spread out like a floral apron, betokened ambition and a measure of prosperity.

She had to stop herself from going up to the front entrance. *Remember who you are now*, an inner voice admonished her. Walking slowly around to the servants' door at the back of the house, she knocked and waited. Knocked again, more loudly. At length the door opened and a small boy, probably about eight or nine years old, stood just inside the threshold. He said nothing but stared at her enquiringly. She gave her name, adding, 'Dr Oram asked me to report here today.' The boy turned wordlessly and disappeared. A minute later he returned, mumbling, 'Mother says you're to come in.' She followed him inside, leaving her large bag in the kitchen. 'This way,' he said.

In the dimly lit parlour, where drawn curtains were failing to keep the midday warmth at bay, a plump woman rose clumsily from an armchair to greet her.

'Ah, Miss Trent,' she said. 'I'm Mrs Oram. Well, it's a relief you've got here in good time, I can tell you. We've been short of help since our housekeeper up and left us more than a week ago, all of a sudden. Most inconvenient. And hard these days to replace domestic servants. So when my husband saw a newspaper notice of your ship's arrival he went straight off to Fremantle to hire a suitable person. Plenty of cleaning to catch up with. Our part-time cook will be here before long to prepare tonight's meal, that's Mrs Leckie, lives five minutes away, husband works on the railway. When she comes in she'll tell you where to put your things, and explain some other practical matters. Meanwhile I'll show you what needs doing around the house. So come with me.'

Mrs Oram conducted her from room to room, prattling about this and that, gesturing at dusty floors and shelves, and describing various tasks. Isabella tried not to let curiosity distract her, but as this was the first time she had been inside any colonial house there were several things that caught her eye: the central arched hallway with its ornate cornices, the pressed-tin patterning on the high ceilings of some rooms, the varnished floorboards made from a red-brown timber that she would later learn to call jarrah, the heavy cast-iron fireplace surround with a carved wooden mantelpiece above it. Would this house ever get cold enough to justify setting a fire? She found it hard to imagine.

A personal question interrupted her musings. 'How old are you, Miss Trent?'

'Twenty-seven.'

'And not married!'

'Widow,' Isabella lied. It felt like the truth.

'Oh. Still, you're pretty and well spoken, so I hope you won't be setting your cap at some local gentleman and leaving us in the lurch.'

'I'm not looking for another husband, I assure you.'

The *Nairnshire* had reached Fremantle just over six weeks after leaving Gravesend, and within another three days she had signed the paperwork for this position in Guildford. Dr Raymond Oram was the first prospective employer to come into the Immigration Depot where Miss Monk waited expectantly with her young charges. 'Like heifers in a cattle yard, ain't we?' grinned

Penny Priddle. Oram spoke quietly to Miss Monk, who then summoned four of the women for interviews, Isabella among them. After questioning each in turn – a perfunctory process – it didn't take him long to offer the job to her. He summarised the housekeeping duties in general terms; she gave a general assurance that she could fulfil them competently. He mentioned the wages and live-in arrangements, asked her to travel to Guildford by rail the following morning, wrote down his address, nodded curtly and left.

'Didn't think much of *him*,' sniffed Ruth Fitch, one of those interviewed. 'Grey beard, grey clothes, grey eyes, grey teeth.'

Isabella shrugged. She didn't much care what sort of person her new employer was, let alone what he looked like. A roof over her head, food and a few shillings to keep body and soul together – that was all she needed for the time being, while trying to work her way towards some meaningful options in the new life she had so rashly chosen.

The next morning she said her goodbyes to the other women, knowing that they would soon disperse. By all accounts, servants were in high demand not only in Fremantle and Perth but also in rural towns and in far corners of this vast but under-populated colony of Western Australia. Isabella felt no personal attachment to other members of her group, and thought it unlikely that she would see them again.

On the point of setting off for the rail station she was drawn aside by Mary Monk, who warmly wished her a happy future. 'I know an uncommonly capable woman when I see one,' she told Isabella. 'My prediction is that you're destined for a higher station in life than domestic service. No doubt you'll attract the notice of a good man before long. I've heard Dr Oram is a respectable figure in Guildford society, and his male acquaintances will surely become aware that he has an intelligent and comely young woman in his household.'

Isabella shook her head in a self-deprecating way. *I don't want that*, she thought, *but you're the one who deserves to settle down with a decent husband, instead of spending all your time as a shipboard matron in charge of waifs and strays.*

As for herself, here she was in a foreign town and an unfamiliar role, learning quickly what a servant's duties involved and beginning to recognise already how little thought she had given to this in the past, through all the years when the ever reliable Perkins was working for Aunt Barbara and then for her. Combining the functions of cook and housemaid, Perkins attended to things quietly and efficiently, making it unnecessary for an employer to pay close attention to what was being done or how. The daily effort that must have gone into it all was hardly discernible to Isabella at the time, but having suddenly come down in the world through her own impetuous decision she could see now how constricted and comfortless a servant's life was.

The menial work took long hours to complete and drained her energy. By the day's end, after scrubbing floors, shaking out rugs, scouring the oven, dusting furniture and rooms, polishing the brass and carrying bucket after bucket of water and slops, she felt bone weary. Other tasks were not so physically onerous but had to be coordinated to fit into the time available. Though Mrs Leckie came at regular points in the day to do the cooking, it was Isabella's responsibility to order food supplies in consultation with both cook and mistress, to ensure that pots, pans, cutlery and plates were cleaned and laid out when required, to attend to tradesmen, and sometimes to hurry to Padbury's Store if an item was urgently needed for larder or table. As her chores settled into a routine and her hands attended to them more automatically, she found that her mind often dwelt on the Gudrun story. Under her breath she recited various passages from Morris's poem, imagining how some of the scenes might be stitched into an old Icelandic counterpane or wall hanging.

Nights seldom brought much rest. She slept fitfully under a single blanket on a narrow sagging stretcher bed in the kitchen, and although the draughts that came in under the back door were welcome on the hottest summer nights, they often left her with an aching neck. Strange sounds startled her, and she would lie awake listening in the darkness. Was that scratching noise outside made by a dog? A rat? Or some unfamiliar animal, perhaps one of the 'possums' she'd heard mentioned but not yet seen? And that occasional warbling by moonlight: what kind of bird could produce something so fluently melodious?

Miss Monk had told the members of her group not to show surprise if their employer invited them to join the rest of the household around the meal table. Some Australians, she said, liked to pretend that there was no social barrier between master and servant. But the Oram family did not make any such inclusive gesture. Mrs Leckie would usually try to set a portion aside for Isabella in the kitchen, and sometimes there were leftovers. She had to feed herself hastily when she could snatch a few minutes between chores.

Yet in other ways she seemed to be treated almost as an equal. Mrs Clarissa Oram had an informal, chatty way of speaking to her, and made it clear she expected Isabella to respond openly. Any servant-to-mistress deference or diffidence was brushed aside. She would often interrupt Isabella's work to ask her opinion about all sorts of things: how best to arrange certain flowers in a large vase, or which kind of plum to use for making jam, or whether a particular new hat was dignified enough to wear to church, or whether the rose bushes should be pruned more severely, or even whether her pair of youngsters had 'become too independent-minded for their own good.'

The two Oram children were away from the house for many hours on end most days of the week attending the local school, and at other times they would usually be playing in the street or, when the weather kept them inside, closeted in their bedroom with some book, some game, some surreptitious pastime. So Isabella had only superficial contact with them, but she saw enough to form a few impressions. The eight-year-old boy, Jimmy, had seemed shy when she encountered him upon her arrival, but his boisterous side emerged when he romped with companions, real or imaginary. She glimpsed him occasionally through the windows as he ran up and down the path, chasing or eluding phantasmal foes, firing finger pistols, wrestling valiantly with invisible creatures.

His ten-year-old sister Emma was quiet and earnest. She had a way of sucking in her top lip until it nearly vanished under the bottom one, and lowering her eyebrows at the same time, seeming to suggest that much of what went on around her deserved her suspicion or downright disapproval. Despite being 'a clever girl' in her mother's proud estimation, Emma had never acquired the art of smiling.

Isabella knew where she stood with the children and their mother, but with Dr Raymond Oram she felt less certain. Although he was usually in the house during the mornings, she saw little of him then because he had appointments with patients in the front room that served as his surgery. In the afternoons, and sometimes in the evenings, he tended to be out and about, either visiting the sick in their own homes or attending a meeting in another of his community roles such as senior churchwarden for St Matthew's. But from time to time there would be a passing encounter in some part of the house: he might come out of his surgery as she was dusting picture frames in the passage, or open the front door to leave as she was sweeping the verandah. At such moments he would nod silently, and then glance at her sidelong, as if he had not quite made up his mind about her. Something in his manner made her uneasy. Was it that he looked, in a certain light, somewhat like her father?

She was getting to know Guildford, particularly the area between Ethel Street and Padbury's Store, which she often traversed because Mrs Oram, pleading a painful hip, generally asked her to do the family's shopping. The quarter-hour walk in each direction took her past the most substantial public build-ings – the Mechanics' Institute, the Courthouse, the Rose and Crown Hotel. In scale and in some of its features the town reminded her of typical large Wiltshire villages, though laid out in a more orderly rectangular manner, with chessboard regularity except for the riverside paths. The Swan and Helena rivers came together not far from the house, and their confluence made the town seem like an island – an island where the alien mingled with the familiar. A few English plants and trees were recognis-able amid local species. The small railway station, her point of arrival here, resembled several stopping places for trains in the countryside she had left behind on the other side of the world: though not remarkably handsome, the station made a confident statement about civic aspirations. Her walks to and from the store also took her past the town square, with an Anglican church at its centre, St Matthew's: orange brick, tall lancet windows, a high pitched roof with brick gables – less impressively designed than the stone church buildings she remembered fondly from Leek, especially St Edward's, but with a measure of parochial dignity nevertheless.

Though expected to attend Sunday morning worship services at St Matthew's with the Oram family, Isabella was off duty on Sunday afternoons, which became a regular opportunity for visits to her neighbour, Mrs Tilly Carter. Widow Carter, a genial soul, had befriended her after an encounter at Padbury's Store during Isabella's first week in the town. It was a relief for Isabella to be able to talk comfortably once a week over afternoon tea, mentioning aspects of her new domicile that amused, vexed or puzzled her.

One of the puzzles was the very fact that she, ostensibly a mere servant, could have this easy sociable interaction with a person of Mrs Carter's independent standing, and could discuss the matter without awkwardness. Having grown up in Essex, the wealthy widow understood Isabella's uncertainty about how to interpret the apparent blurring of class distinctions out here in the colony. They both knew well how remote the position occupied by people of property in England was from that of servants and labourers. Tilly laughed heartily when Isabella recited from memory Bernard Shaw's witty précis in the Fabian manifesto: 'Land and capital have created the division of society into hostile classes, with large appetites and no dinners at one extreme and large dinners and no appetites at the other.'

'Oh yes. Different picture in this part of the world,' said Tilly, 'and a good thing, too. Talent and hard work gain more respect than so-called high birth. Look at some of the leading lights here in Guildford. Walter Padbury, very successful businessman, elected a couple of years ago as our first mayor, came to the colony as a penniless orphan. Or there's Alfred Letch, richest man in Western Australia I'm told, Perth City Councillor, who used to own the Perth to Guildford coach service – he was shipped out as a convict. People like that don't forget who they used to be, and don't put themselves above other folk. Mind you, I wouldn't say the same of everyone in this town.'

TWENTY

*T*HE MIDSUMMER WEATHER BECAME OPPRESSIVE AND weeks went by with hardly a drop of rain. Isabella found the day's duties more and more gruelling. The air within the house accumulated warmth and would not cool down. As she toiled over all the vigorous cleaning, sweeping and polishing, sweat ran into her eyes, along her arms and down her back. Her hair, which had darkened since she left England, felt lank. Her shoulders ached. The harsh soap made her hands itch. In the street it was even more unpleasant, and not only because of the inescapable heat. She could not accustom herself to being assaulted by the fierce sunlight. Her light bonnet did little to protect her from the glare. Each time she stepped outside, a sudden brightness slapped her and before she had walked more than a few yards towards Padbury's Store her eyes were feeling bruised.

'Everything in the garden is shrivelling up,' she told Tilly. 'And there's hardly a blade of green grass to be seen anywhere. Birds have gone quiet, too. Losing heart, I suppose. Does this happen here every summer? This scorching? The town seems to be turning into an arid wasteland. A kind of desert.'

'My dear, I assure you it can get much more parched than this, if you travel inland into the hills and beyond. I once journeyed up towards York with my husband Fred in a rattletrap during late summer, when there was a terrible drought. Some business matter, I forget why he wanted to go up there. Well, it was like wandering into hell. Hotter than you can imagine, a furnace, with smoke on the horizon from a bushfire that looked to be heading our way. Dead sheep in dusty paddocks; I can't forget the sight or smell of them. Fred turned the horses around and we came straight back home.'

Picturing the desolate countryside described by Tilly, Isabella remembered William Morris's account of parts of the Icelandic landscape he once travelled through – another kind of barren wilderness, much of it covered by volcanic detritus. Odd to think that Australia and Iceland, so different in other ways, could both produce vast tracts of wasteland, whether seared by fiery eruptions from underground or by sunburnt air and flaming bush.

Returning from Tilly's place to the Oram house, she felt troubled by the sheer strangeness of this physical environment. Much of it, to her eyes, would remain outlandish. Yet there were sights to cherish, too. The colours of birds fascinated her, especially parrots. She recalled the lines in *Sir Gawain* depicting a scarf that adorned the hero's helmet, brightly embroidered with popinjays. And there now, taking off at startling speed from a fence right beside her as she walked, was a pair of these brilliantly vivid creatures, parrots with emerald green body, yellow collar and red forehead, so swift in their flight and so rapidly veering that they looked like a token of freedom in all directions.

A token that would prove to be delusive.

Sometimes menace will not announce itself until the last moment. Dissembling, it can creep up gradually and unobtrusively. Although Guildford's blazing sunshine would persist for months, something shadowy was encroaching sidelong on the edges of Isabella's daylight world. What soon began to happen would seem, when she looked back on it afterwards, like the stealthy onset of darkness, a hardly perceptible crepuscular change followed by a sudden fearful recognition that night had fallen around her and she could find no way out of it.

As time went by, Raymond Oram appeared to become less reticent towards her. Their encounters were still infrequent, and his manner generally remained watchful, but she sensed a slight loosening of reserve, though awkwardness hovered. On one occasion she was down on all fours, bent over, stretching forward to scrub the floor with her dress rucked up around her knees, when Oram unexpectedly entered the room behind her. 'Ah. Good Morning, Miss Trent,' he said. Clambering to her feet she returned his greeting, conscious of her flushed and sweaty face. She tucked loose strands of hair under her cap. He stood there for a minute or two, shifting from one foot to another, murmuring a few clumsy phrases. Bemused, Isabella could not see where this odd little conversation was leading. Then, turning suddenly on his heel, he left the room.

A couple of weeks after that, as she was washing dishes, he came into the kitchen for the first time since her arrival. Surprise made her fumble with a plate before wiping her hands on the apron. She gave him an enquiring look.

'Ah. Interrupting your work,' he observed needlessly. 'I just… the thought came to me that perhaps something is affecting your health.'

'Oh? I don't believe so. Why do you say that?'

'You're noticeably thinner than when I hired you a few months ago. Not feeling unwell in any way?'

'Not particularly, no. The work is quite tiring, and I don't always sleep soundly.'

'No loss of appetite?'

'I eat what I can when I can.' *Snatching food on the run*, she wanted to say. *That's the way it is for a servant.*

'Hmm. Well, do let me know if you feel in need of tonics. I could prescribe a digestive remedy. There are herbal infusions…' His voice trailed off. He coughed and retreated, leaving her to frown at the soapy water.

But as autumn gave way to winter she began to feel a stabbing sensation beneath her ribs. Had she strained a muscle in her back with all the lifting and bending? Or could it be a problem in her chest – an inflammation of the lungs? The Oram children had recently been confined to bed with heavy colds and hacking coughs. Though they were back at school now, perhaps she had picked up an infection from them, which may have turned into pleurisy. The nights were colder and the draughty kitchen was an increasingly uncomfortable place to sleep. When she turned over in her narrow bed the sharp pain made her gasp. Despite having responded dismissively to Dr Oram's earlier questions about her health, she knew she had been losing weight, which may have weakened her, she supposed, and made her suscep-tible to ailments.

So early one afternoon, when he came into the hallway as she was dusting the picture rail there, she asked if she might have the benefit of his medical advice.

'Of course, of course.' He ushered her into his office, and she explained the symptoms.

'Ah. Hard to tell. Could be the lungs. I need to listen closely to your breathing.' He picked up his stethoscope. 'Remove the apron, please, and unbutton your bodice.'

Spoken in a matter-of-fact tone of almost fatherly authority, his instruction could hardly be disobeyed, though she felt a slight qualm as he stood close in front of her, staring while she undid the buttons. Then, leaning in towards her with a wooden tube in his hand, he placed one end of it near her heart and the other end to his ear. 'Inhale deeply.' As she breathed in and out she saw his shoulders rise and fall too, and heard a shuddering kind of sigh. He put the stethoscope aside, parted the bodice further with a quick movement and put his ear directly against her bosom. She stiffened and pulled back. This was much too intimate. She felt an upsurge of panic, suddenly aware that they were alone in the house: the morning's patients had left, Mrs Oram was in Perth for the day to visit her sister, the children were at school, and the cook would not be due for another hour or more.

Gripping her shoulder with one bony hand, Oram tried with the other to cup one of her breasts. She recoiled. 'No! What are you doing?' All pretence abandoned, he pushed her hard against the wall, pinioned her, tugged her bodice roughly open to the waist, tore loose part of the undergarment. Angry and frightened, she cried out. With its thick curtains and rugs the house soaked up the sound. The harder she struggled the more tightly he held her. His wrist was pressing into her throat now, his elbow rubbing against one of her exposed nipples, his knee lifted high between her thighs. 'Keep still, damn you!' he grunted.

Desperately resisting, she kicked at his leg, twisted sharply sideways and managed somehow to wriggle from his grasp. As she staggered from the room he lunged at her but she struck his arm away fiercely with her fist, flung open the front door and ran half-naked down the path and out into the street, yelling and sobbing. She fled past an astonished elderly couple walking slowly arm in arm, who turned with mouths agape to see this mad dishevelled creature rush into a nearby yard where an older woman held out rescuing arms.

Tilly, picking a bunch of geraniums beside her front verandah, had heard a shrill cry and looked up to see her friend running frantically from the next-door house into the street. The sounds that came from Isabella were like those of a stricken animal, and her eyes were as wild as a maenad's, but the most startling thing was the indecent disarray of her clothing. Tilly opened a gate and the young woman hurried through, distraught, throwing her arms around her neighbour's neck, weeping and shaking.

She sat for more than an hour in Tilly's parlour sipping tea, wiping her eyes, a large warm shawl covering her semi-naked-ness. Tilly listened and nodded and made another pot of tea as Isabella talked on and on, at first in a passionate, febrile way and then after a while more calmly. At length the words and sniffling stopped altogether and Isabella bowed her head, exhausted; but her sense of utter relief at having escaped was short-lived. There was a knock at the door. Tilly opened it cautiously. A police sergeant stood there, asking to see Miss Trent.

During the days that followed, kept in custody and repeat-edly questioned, she came to see that her plight was far worse than she had first thought. She had not eluded her employer's clutches after all. It transpired that, moving quickly to forestall any accusations she might make, he had gone straight to the police station while she was sheltering in Tilly Carter's parlour, and lodged a formal complaint, alleging that she had behaved scandalously and fallen into a fit of hysterical lunacy. When the sergeant revealed this story in the course of his questioning, her indignation quickly turned into a frenzy of distress. Tilly Carter came to the police station and was allowed to sit with Isabella for a few minutes, holding her hand, but could find nothing consoling to say.

'Surely they'll believe in my innocence!' Isabella cried out. 'What he says is so preposterous!' And then a further alarming thought: 'But when I'm released, what then? How will it be possible for me to get work elsewhere without a letter of recommendation from him?'

Noticing a momentary twitch of Tilly's eyebrows at the mention of release, Isabella began for the first time to consider that his version, not hers, might be upheld. Would that mean imprisonment? And even if not, how would she support herself from now on in any case? Wherever the path ahead might go, it would take her into deeper darkness.

A small measure of hope arrived on the third day in the shape of a very short man with a very large moustache who introduced himself as Inspector Rowe. The local police sergeant had asked him, Rowe explained, to see whether he could provide some help in this matter. The glance she darted at him was full of mistrust. 'Help?' she said sceptically. 'Help for me?' Spreading his hands in a gesture that could have been part shrug and part gentle encouragement, Rowe said simply, 'Tell me about the incident. Your side of the story.'

Her response was voluble, and she could hear it rising shrilly as she insisted that she was blameless, that her employer had made a crude attempt to take advantage of her and all she had done was to resist strenuously his violent assault. She described the circumstances and recounted in detail what had taken place.

Rowe listened intently. When she paused for breath he asked a quiet question, an unexpected and seemingly trivial one, at a tangent to what she had been telling him.

'I think I can hear the Midlands in your voice,' he said. 'Am I right?'

Disconcerted, she stared at him. 'What relevance could that have? How does it help anything?'

'Probably neither relevant nor helpful,' he admitted with an apologetic air. 'Listening to your voice makes me feel homesick, that's all. I grew up in the Potteries myself. Tunstall. But that was long ago. And you?'

'Just a few miles upbank from Tunstall,' she said. 'Leek was where I lived. I've been away from there for nearly ten years.'

There was a pause. She looked at him charily. His expression was sad but she thought she detected something compassionate in it. 'After what's happened here,' she blurted out, 'I almost wish I'd never left my home town.'

'Family still there?'

'All gone.'

'Alone in the world, then.'

It didn't sound like a question, so she gave no reply at first; but as he seemed to be waiting she added impulsively, 'The solitary life doesn't frighten me, Inspector. The people I loved most are either dead or so far away that they might as well be. I don't want to replace them.'

He nodded, frowned and examined the back of his hand. Sensing that he was sympathetic, she voiced her worries about the difficulty of finding a new position without a letter of support from Oram. Rowe advised her to put such thoughts aside for the time being. A magistrate would hear her case the next day, he told her, and the most important thing for her was to concentrate on keeping calm during that process, giving a clear account of the plain facts of the matter.

It did not turn out like that. Oram made his statement first, asserting that she had suddenly attempted to seduce him and then, when he firmly rejected her improper advances, had lapsed into a kind of crazed tantrum, a paroxysm, ripping her own clothes and raving wildly. On the basis of his 'long-established medical expertise,' he testified that her nervous system was evidently in the grip of a serious illness. The extreme nature of her lewd behaviour and emotional convulsions indicated, he said, a disorder of the womb.

By the time the magistrate asked her with stern disdain whether she had any response to the charge of gross public indecency, Isabella was trembling uncontrollably, enraged by Oram's mendacity. As she gripped the rail in front of her and began to speak, threatening shadows crowded into the corners of the room. Or of her mind. Although she tried to give an orderly summary of what had happened to her, phrases tangled shapelessly in her mouth and she heard her voice rising, cracking, squawking. Then heavy sobs shook her and she could not continue.

Inspector Rowe was called on next, but could make only brief remarks. The defendant, he said, had spoken quite rationally about the incident when he interviewed her. Though she was obviously discomposed at the present moment, this need not indicate any underlying mental instability. Given an opportunity to make a fresh start with another employer, she was capable, in his view, of carrying out her duties respectfully and reliably.

The magistrate soon arrived at his finding: Dr Oram had been the victim of an episode of unprovoked hysteria on the part of his housekeeper; Inspector Rowe's opinion was more charitable than convincing; Miss Trent's version of events, with its quite improbable and indeed libellous tale of assault by a leading citizen of Guildford, confirmed that she was completely deranged. She should be committed forthwith to the Fremantle Asylum, the length of her time there to be determined by the Medical Superintendent.

Straight after the proceedings concluded, Tilly Carter approached Rowe outside the building, tears in her eyes. 'It seems so terribly unjust to me,' she said. 'And I think you may share my view. Can nothing be done for her?'

He sighed dejectedly. 'It's an unfortunate outcome, Mrs Carter. But in my position I can't publicly question the verdict. I can only hope the Superintendent will decide not to keep her immured for long. Hope must wrestle with expectation. Though asylums are supposed to be places of refuge, I fear the one in Fremantle is generally easier to get into than out of. Much will depend on how she conducts herself there. I wish I could keep an eye on the situation, but my period of leave is up. I'm due to return to Geraldton tomorrow. You'll visit her from time to time?'

'Of course I will. Regularly.'

TWENTY-ONE

*A*s they set out on foot from the Fremantle railway station, cold westerly gusts stirred up gritty dust around them. 'This way,' said the laconic young constable, jabbing the air with his thumb. Though he had spoken only a few words on the journey from Guildford, his manner was not unfriendly.

'How far?' Having eaten little for a couple of days, Isabella felt lightheaded and weak. There was a tremor in her limbs. Sand underfoot made it hard to keep her balance.

He shrugged. 'A bit of a trudge.' Slackening his pace, he reached out an open hand. 'I'll take your bag.' She gave it to him with a grateful smile.

After a while they turned a corner and the road rose gradually towards the northeast. He pointed uphill at their destination: a large well-proportioned structure, resembling from a distance a stony-faced English manor house that moderated its Gothic Revival gestures with solemn restraint. As they were approaching it she stopped in a patch of shade to get her breath back, and glanced apprehensively at the high enclosing wall capped with chunks of jagged rock. Like the tall structure inside it, the pale-grey wall was made from pocked limestone. Behind a clump of grass near the grim entrance gate something shuffled, and they saw a large brown-winged bird, white in body and head but with the dark hooked beak of a raptor. It was dragging an injured wing.

'Osprey,' said the constable. 'In the wrong place here, poor wretch. Belongs near water. Won't last long on the ground, anyhow, wounded like that.'

Five minutes later, having countersigned her admission document, he left Isabella and her bag of clothes with the Matron, who introduced herself as Mrs Higgs.

'Well, Miss Trent,' she said briskly. 'I won't try to explain everything at once. It's going to take you some while to get accustomed to this place and the way we do things here. So for now I'll just mention a few practical matters…' She gave Isabella a quick summary of the strict rules for inmates, the meal-table procedure, the daily timetable of activities, and the sleeping arrangements. Most of the beds were in a large dormitory, the Matron explained, but there were also a few individual cells, one of which would be assigned initially to Isabella because the dormitory was full.

Conducted down high-ceilinged corridors towards her cell, she felt cold sweat on her face and neck. Her eyeballs were aching and the tremor had come back into her arms and legs. She put a hand out to steady herself against the wall, but stumbled.

'What's the matter, lass?' The Matron looked at her closely. 'You've gone deathly pale. Drop your bag there and take my arm.' She helped her a little way further along and stopped at an open wooden door. 'Here's your cell now,' she said. 'Lie down on the bed there.' She put a hand on Isabella's clammy forehead. 'Fever.'

The illness lasted for days, which passed in a febrile blur of shivering, vomiting, and ugly dreaming. Faces of the remembered dead arraigned her, reproached her, condemned her. When at last the nauseous waves ebbed away she felt exhausted.

'My dear, you look so wretchedly thin,' said Tilly Carter when she visited later that week.

'I can't get warm. My cell's always damp. I've asked for another blanket but they say it's not allowed.'

'I'll speak to the Matron. She's a reasonable person, I think. Perhaps she'll let me fetch something warm for you.'

The next time she came, Tilly brought a large parcel. 'If anything can keep you snug at night, this will,' she told Isabella. 'Special permission of the Matron. It served my late husband well. Don't open it until you're back in your cell. It's to be kept there discreetly and not mentioned to other patients.'

Unwrapping the parcel later, Isabella found it contained a man's frock coat. The woollen broadcloth, spread over her like a blanket during the night, made her feel warm for the first time since entering the Asylum. Yet the nocturnal hours remained difficult. As if forsaken in a vast tract of darkness she lay there restlessly, unable to push from her mind the stark images of harrowing dispossession. *Perhaps it will always be like this*, said an inner voice. She feared being forever fastened to what she had lost. Sewn tightly into her accumulated grief at the bereavements, the squandered loves, the relinquished longings. Bound with wiry stitching to every misfortune, every injustice and every bitter irony that had disfigured her life.

Between each dawn and dusk there were routines that made it easier to forget such things for a while. Meals gave the day its basic shape, and what they offered was as predictable as their timing. For breakfast, two ounces of oatmeal, six ounces of bread with butter, and one pint of tea with sugar and milk. For dinner, six ounces of meat (or occasionally fish), twelve ounces of vegetables and five ounces of bread – with something sweet twice a week: rice pudding on Wednesdays, plum pudding on Sundays. Every morning brought its regular chores, the most arduous being the scrubbing of floorboards. After that, the attendants liked to shepherd all patients outdoors during good weather, reducing the need for close supervision. Some of the women would spend whole afternoons just sitting stone-like on the broad steps that led down to the lumpy lawns, lost in their reveries. Others devised girlish games with skipping ropes or rubber balls to while away the time, or wandered aimlessly around the shrub-fringed garden enclosure in small muttering groups. In the evenings and on wet days they could play with packs of cards or with draught boards. A few chose books from the small library collection, and this was Isabella's preferred pastime. Happening on a copy of *The Woman in White*, she read Wilkie Collins's novel with increasing absorption, drawn along by every twist of the story. Some passages reminded her poignantly of her aunt's immurement at Ticehurst; others made her reflect on her own grim situation here.

Sinking into that fictional world was one way of trying to calm her mind, though with limited success. Sinking into the daily routine of insipid meals and dreary tasks was another. When not caught up in those distracting activities, Isabella made an effort to quell her distress so that she could start to think rationally about advancing her prospects of release. The outcome of the Guildford hearing had been a double shock: to have her account of the assault curtly rejected, and then to be sent off to this Asylum for an indefinite period of detention – it was all so utterly inequitable that she was continually gripped by a wild fist-clenching rage, and had to subdue the impulse to smash a window, hurl a water-jug to the floor or strike at somebody. Any such outburst, she knew, would only make things worse. She must concentrate on whatever might help to free her from this place as soon as possible. She would talk about it when Tilly next came to visit her. Seek her advice and assistance.

Meanwhile she had to submit meekly to all the indignities of being held here. Be thankful for small mercies, she told herself, knowing that the administrative system had compassionate intentions. Affixed to a wall of the dining room was a framed sheet listing *Rules for the Guidance of Attendants, Fremantle Lunatic Asylum* above the name of a previous superintendent, Colonial Surgeon H. Calvert Barnett, and the date July 1st 1872. The statement was headed by three worthy principles: 'Gentleness. Firmness. Truthfulness.' Well, Isabella could acknowledge that Matron Higgs did embody those kind-hearted ways of treating people, and for the most part the orderlies seemed amicable enough, if sometimes coarse. But they could hardly ensure that the women in their care showed gentle, firm or truthful attributes.

There were nearly fifty patients in the female wing of the building, separated from the more numerous group of male inmates whose voices often floated over the tall thick dividing wall. Many of the women had little to do with one another, keeping to themselves even during meals. Their reclusiveness matched Isabella's withdrawn mood. Without needing to get into much conversation she could see that they were a motley assortment of the frail, the destitute, the wayward and the feebleminded. In general she took scant notice of their names or individual peculiarities, but after a while a few of them caught her attention.

She first became aware of Sally Litchfield when she heard a snivelling noise opposite her at the midday dinner table, and looked up to see tears running down the cheeks of a listless young woman. The next afternoon she noticed her again, sitting on the steps above the open grassed area, rubbing her swollen legs, crying and babbling to herself. She was about Isabella's own age. As the sunlight fell on her she appeared to be crouching over the shadow she cast. The words dribbling from her mouth formed a penitential prayer. 'Dear Jesus, pardon me Jesus, forgive me my trespasses, my many many dreadful trespasses, oh Jesus, lead me not into temptation, not again, please deliver me, deliver me...' Isabella overheard one attendant say to another, 'Silly Sally needs another purgative.'

Much more placid and girlish than Sally was Emma Dodds, who gave her age as '18 next birthday' and wore a vague smile all day long. As time slipped by, Isabella noticed that young Emma had become increasingly stout. It was no surprise to hear from wash-house gossip that the Superintendent had examined this hapless girl, 'in Matron's presence, of course,' and confirmed that she was pregnant. Before being admitted to the Asylum she had been accosted, so the whisper went, on her way home from church by a man who promised to marry her and then led her into the bush. As far as Isabella could see, Emma was unaware of her condition until, a few weeks later, a child was delivered and quickly removed from the Asylum, taking the girl's fixed smile with her.

There was one woman who tried to sit next to Isabella at every meal and follow her almost everywhere. Janet Woolner, about the age of 50, insisted plaintively that she was Isabella's mother. Nobody took this seriously; it was known that in the past she had made the same claim on another patient, and doubtful that she had ever been a mother to anyone. Janet Woolner's misery expressed itself through self-punishment: she would sometimes beat her own unsuckled breasts in a desperate fury.

Everyone gave Filthy Betty Philp a wide berth. Her language and gestures were foul; her snarling complaints were constant. She masturbated without concealment, tore up her clothes, flung her excrement about the corridors, and kept removing her stockings to throw them over the garden wall. She often got into scuffles for no particular reason except that she seemed to enjoy fighting and biting. People said Filthy Betty had physically threatened the Matron several times, and Isabella once came upon her trying to choke an assistant. She was often held in restraints for days in one of the refractory cells.

The orderlies referred to some patients tersely as 'chronic imbeciles.' Tilly Carter, arriving for one of her regular visits, saw two of them wrestling playfully on the ground like puppies. 'Idiotic but harmless, poor things,' she said to Isabella. Alice Bradley was a notable example: plump as a pumpkin, prone to fits, she had once hidden herself (so the story went) in the Matron's water closet, curled up under the seat.

On an evening when entertainment came to the Asylum, Isabella's hopes of early release were suddenly smothered.

Patients had rearranged the dining-room furniture to create a seating area for themselves and clear a performance area for the pair of musicians. Orderlies stood on either side of the room, ready to intervene if behaviour got out of hand. The hum of anticipation subsided as the Matron ushered in two men carrying their instruments, a portly bewhiskered fiddler and a much younger, leaner, smooth-cheeked concertina player. Beaming benevolently, Mrs Higgs addressed the group: 'Ladies,' she said, 'we are fortunate indeed to have these performers here tonight to entertain us with their musicianship. There will be some well-known tunes, so if you like to join in with singing and dancing you may do so, but I expect you all to be on your very best behaviour. Try not to get over-excited. Now please give a welcome to these visitors, my cousin Cyril Higgs and his son Jem.'

As scattered applause died away, the duo launched into the strains of Australia's nearest approximation to a national song: 'There is a land where summer skies / Are gleaming with a thousand dyes...' They played with more gusto than polish, disguising the defects of their instrumentation with the volume of their voices. A popular shanty followed: 'As I was a-walking down Paradise Street / Way hey blow the man down...' Janet Woolner and a few of the other women sang along uncertainly. And then came a maudlin funereal song, which took Isabella back to a conversation long ago with Julius Kendrick, when he told her it was a favourite ditty in his regimental mess hall: 'Wrap me up in my tarpaulin jacket / And say a poor buffer lies low...' The visiting musicians were producing a raucous rendition, but behind it she imagined she could hear the vibrancy of Kendrick's distinctive voice, forgetting for the moment that it had been permanently silenced.

The performance turned next to dance tunes – reels, polkas, waltzes. Some of the women stood up and began to dance, singly or with one another, shyly at first and then boisterously. Isabella held back, troubled by fragments of memory. She closed her eyes – but soon someone was nudging her in the back and chuckling. Turning, she found that Alice Bradley had come up behind her. Alice reached out her hand to fondle Isabella's hair. Clasped her clumsily around the waist. Started to jig in a buffoonish way. Stopped abruptly. Tried to give her a slobbering kiss on the mouth.

Panic flooded Isabella's body. With a yell of protest, she shoved the woman violently back and struck at her, knocking her over. Others ran towards them and a melee broke out, with punching and kicking, much of it done in fear by Isabella. Alice, as she fell, had hit her head on a table leg and was bleeding profusely from a scalp wound. One eye was already puffing up. 'Let's get a bandage on that deep cut,' said Matron Higgs, and led the whimpering Alice away. Two orderlies held Isabella tightly by the arms, tried without success to calm her, and took her to one of the refractory cells. There, over the next week, she learnt that she had now been formally classified as 'dangerous, and given to bouts of raving mania.'

The Matron was not only reproachful but also puzzled.

'When you first arrived here, Miss Trent,' she said, 'there was a good deal of sympathy for you. For my own part, I doubted that you were capable of the unprovoked wildness that Dr Collins accused you of showing. But I must say that this fierce attack on Alice Bradley looks to be a similar outburst. You surely know that she is just a simpleton who means no harm. Why on earth did you act so savagely towards her?'

Isabella could give no answer. Her rage had already waned, but although she was becoming quiet and rational again, she knew full well that her unpredictable behaviour would seem a sufficient rationale for continuing to incarcerate her in a solitary cell. If the Matron and the Superintendent now regarded this place as her proper domicile for an indefinite period, she could hardly blame them. After all, she herself could see no justification for what she had done, and at this stage she had only the merest inkling of an explanation.

TWENTY-TWO

*A*LMOST IMPERCEPTIBLY, DAYS SLID INTO WEEKS. Months into years. Ordinary measures of elapsed time no longer meant very much; for Isabella it was one prolonged ordeal. The only passage markers apart from her dull daily routines were the infrequent special events.

Whenever the Higgs pair of musicians returned for one of their annual performances she was confined to her cell – 'precautionary detention,' an orderly told her, 'to avoid any repeat of the trouble you caused.' From the darkness of her little room she heard without regret the scraping fiddle, the wheezing concertina and snatches of rowdy song. If she found herself beginning to think about the dancing episode and her explosive reaction to Alice's embrace she pushed it all hurriedly out of her mind.

Occasionally there was music of a different sort. Every Christmas season a few earnest local parishioners would stand in the yard to sing carols. Their singing was so sleepily slow that it transformed the message: 'tidings of comfort and joy' turned into a series of dreary lamentations. The same little church group came back again on Easter Sundays, valiantly attempting to raise up their voices in accord with the jubilant sentiments of the season's hymns.

Each New Year's Eve a festive air permeated the whole Asylum. This was the only time when men from the other wing were allowed to mix with their female counterparts. Admonished beforehand and closely supervised by an augmented contingent of warders, the men looked uneasy, even bashful, as they were led into the yard of the women's section. Dancing was the main activity of the evening, but very few of the steppers showed themselves to be nimble. Most of them, men and women alike, moved awkwardly and conversed hesitantly. Though Isabella stood back in a shadowy alcove, manifesting bored disengagement, four men lumbered up in turn to ask her for a dance. All were firmly refused. 'Beggin your pardon, Ma'am, but why won't you?' ventured one bold fellow. Shaking her head vehemently, she gave no answer. While couples circled the room in a plodding schottische or a shuffling waltz, and quartets paced stiffly through a set of the lancers, she eyed them all askance. Grotesque antics, she thought, aware that her disdainful attitude was obvious and must seem excessive to the orderly who stood nearby keeping a wary watch on her.

More frequent visitors, ignored by most of the residents, were the various chaplains who conducted weekly prayers for those wanting to attend. Sally Litchfield was said to be the only regular supplicant. Parents, brothers, sisters, husbands and friends also visited, some often, some seldom. The sole person who came to see Isabella was Tilly. She arrived faithfully once a fortnight, taking the train from Guildford to Fremantle and back in all weathers. Their conversation, never wide-ranging, tended to traverse the same few topics, carefully avoiding others. Tilly made no mention of her neighbours the Orams. Isabella longed to talk without inhibition about her past, about the series of misadventures and impetuous choices that had led her repeatedly to rush from smoke into fire; but there would be too many things to divulge, too much secretiveness to relinquish, and she could never quite bring herself to begin.

One day Tilly reported to her that, having again asked the Matron what stood in the way of Isabella's release, she had received a plainer answer than before. There were two apparent obstacles: Isabella, known to be capable of 'ferocious tantrums,' was regarded by Superintendent Whittle as a danger to other people, and Dr Oram, known to be a close friend of the Superintendent, was presumably exerting private pressure to extend her custody.

Isabella gave a sharp despairing cry. 'So to all intents and purposes I'll be imprisoned here – indefinitely! Like some vicious malefactor! Yet I'm guiltless, you know that, Tilly.'

'My poor dear…' Tilly searched for a consoling word. 'I can hardly imagine the prospect, for an innocent person, of a life behind locked doors. A piteous plight.'

'But it's not pity I want! I refuse to be pitied! I will not let anyone regard me as a pathetic wretch!'

As time dawdled along, two things provided Isabella intermittently with some consolation. Though neither could alleviate her seething sense of being deeply wronged, both enabled her to create an inviolate refuge into which, now and then, she might retreat for a while. One of these consoling resources was her repertoire of precise memories; the other was her flair for needlework design. Eventually the two would come together.

She had always been able to recall details from the past with exceptional accuracy. A few of these were of a kind that could be shared readily enough: in the Guildford days she sometimes used to regale Tilly with descriptions of people who had travelled in her emigrant party, calling to mind not just their distinctive facial features but also this or that individual accent, gait, mannerism. She related incidents from the voyage as well, like the suicide of a young man who vaulted overboard after handing his pocket watch to the bosun. But much else, remembered with equal clarity, she had no wish to talk about to anyone. She thought of these undisclosed items as hanging privately on the walls of her mental gallery. Some of them were cherished visual memories. Some were events and choices that had altered her life's pathway, narrowing or widening it, brightening it or clouding it over.

Miscellaneous things around her in the Asylum would sometimes bring to mind bygone scenes, vanished objects. As she paused at the head of the main staircase, looking down into the sunlit yard through diamantine windowpanes, an earlier image came to her: the recurrent lozenge motif around the edge of an embroidered coverlet that was part of the Icelandic textile display seen in London years before. She remembered exactly the particulars of that pattern, from the medallions in its border to the symmetrically placed human figures with animal masks, like dancing mummers.

At times it felt as if her mind moved high above far-distant landscapes as quietly as a gliding raptor, or hung there in a hover to interpret some small recollection. Beside all the pictorial memories that she held dear there was, as well, the reverberation of powerful language. Many spoken words, conversational fragments, kept echoing in her head. They included a scatter of Aunt Barbara's sagely ironic remarks, enthusiastic pronouncements from members of the Morris circle, witty aphorisms by Bernard Shaw, and heartfelt phrases that had momentarily crossed the formal gap separating her from Julius Kendrick. But written words, too, had left a strong imprint, and her thoughts turned especially now to the book shaped by William Morris from an Icelandic saga, given to her by May, and read avidly during the sea voyage: *The Lovers of Gudrun*. Although Isabella had entrusted her copy of it to Tilly for safekeeping, the story's tragic structure still lingered in her imagination and she had read certain passages so often that she knew them by heart.

Remembrance, with all its stings and solaces, began to merge into Isabella's other inner resource, her talent for elaborate needlework. Since leaving London she had reluctantly put this cherished artistry aside. It belonged to her previous existence, her hidden Lucy world, and in adopting a new role she needed to pretend that she could summon no more than the rudimentary sewing skills of an ordinary domestic servant. But such abnegation had meant relinquishing an important part of who she really was; and now, by chance, she was given an opportunity to take in hand her tattered threadbare selfhood, stitch it back together and embellish it with crafty traceries.

The change came about unexpectedly. One bleak afternoon, steady rain having kept everybody indoors, Isabella was walking along a draughty corridor with arms folded for warmth and head lowered pensively. Tilly Carter, loyal as ever, had been to visit her again that day despite the weather, chattering on for an hour before giving her a benevolent pat on the wrist as she left for the railway station. The old woman's constancy brought Isabella close to tears, and her departure induced a dejected mood.

Someone called out from further down the corridor. 'There you are!'

Isabella looked up enquiringly as the Matron bustled towards her, wagging a finger. 'I hear you've been hiding your light under a bushel, Miss Trent!'

'Oh?'

'Keeping quiet about a certain special skill. Mrs Carter tells me you're a very accomplished needleworker.'

'Whatever made her mention that?'

'Ah, you see, I detained her for a moment as she was leaving here this afternoon – such a kind and pleasant woman, we always like to exchange a few words when she's coming or going – and I happened to tell her that Mrs Samson, a lady from the big new house along the road here, has been wanting to find someone who can undertake embroidery work for domestic furnishings. Well, Tilly Carter said to me at once, "Young Isabella Trent is a gifted embroiderer, you know!" But how would I have known that? You've kept it hidden.'

Isabella shrugged.

'Now, being Irish, you see,' the Matron went on, 'Mrs Samson is particularly fond of a certain kind of stitching from her homeland. It's called Mount… Mount something…'

'Mountmellick,' said Isabella.

'That's it! Mountmellick. All white, she said.'

'Yes, I know it well,' said Isabella. 'Delicate floral patterns. Knotted thread.'

'You're proficient in that technique, then?'

Isabella nodded.

'Well, I'm sure Mrs Samson would be delighted if you'd produce a few pieces for her. Cushion covers, things like that, she wants. She'd provide the materials, thread and so forth, and pay for your work, of course. You could have the earnings put aside to claim when you're released, and meanwhile there'd be the satisfaction of exercising your skills…'

So an arrangement was quickly set up. The Matron, pleased that one of her charges could perform this practical service for a prominent local family, encouraged her to spend a few hours daily on her sewing instead of having to loiter outside with other inmates. Mrs Samson reportedly admired the 'excellent' quality of the embroidered cushion covers, and soon sent two personal garments, a christening gown and a nightdress, to be decorated in the same style. For Isabella this work proved to be a welcome distraction from the despondency that had clung to her. Mastering the intricacies of the Mountmellick method presented a challenge that demanded intense concentration and gave her a gratifying sense that her time in this desolate place was not entirely meaningless.

Yet after a couple of months the task began to feel tedious. It wasn't the needlework itself that palled; it was the absence of any colouring. Mountmellick embroidery was so uniformly pallid – white cotton on white cotton – that its sheer blankness came to seem like an image of her bleached life in this Asylum. Isabella was overwhelmed by a sudden craving for variegated colours, and found herself bringing forth an assortment of them from the storehouse of memory. Her inward eye could picture the delicate patterning and velvet nap of the drapes in her bedroom at the Swindon villa, the minutiae of stitch selection for items toiled over at the Art Needlework School, the chiaroscuro effect of late afternoon light falling across a wall hanging in Kelmscott House, the swathes of dyed cloth stretched out in the sun at the Merton Abbey Works.

Mundane piecework commissioned by the wife of a prosperous merchant was a far cry from the independent artistry that Isabella had once dreamt of achieving. So she would do no more work at another person's bidding, she decided. Instead she would create something for her own satisfaction, something colourful and richly storied. She would select certain visual ideas that had appealed to her, extending them and adding invented details. Little by little the frock coat given her as a blanket could be transformed into an embroidered emblem of the curious life that she had lived and the losses that she had suffered.

This must be a secret project, worked on at nighttime in the privacy of her cell, without the knowledge of other inmates or any officers. Each morning she would turn the coat inside out and leave it on her bed as if it still served simply as a sombre counterpane. What she intended to create could not even be explained to Tilly, who might take offence at the idea that her late husband's garment, donated for its physical comfort, was being converted into something strangely different. Nevertheless she would need Tilly's practical help: the more she thought about the long labour that this undertaking would involve, the more clearly she saw that its execution would depend on a steady but discreet supply of various threads, needles, pieces of cloth, far exceeding in quantity and quality anything that the Matron could be asked to provide. Isabella was sure that Tilly would happily obtain the necessary items and smuggle them to her during weekly visits, without becoming inquisitive about the particular things being sewn. She would just be glad that her young friend had found an activity to distract her from her miserable situation.

At the start, with only a few general intuitions about what she would design and to what purpose, Isabella often sat musing for hours at a time without threading a needle, merely trying to envisage how different elements of a possible encompassing design might fit together in a way that was aesthetically pleasing while also signifying certain aspects of her past life. She wanted somehow – but exactly how? – to draw on, incorporate or adapt some features of textile patterns that she had seen or worked on in London: particular figures and fabrics, particular needlework styles. Crisscrossing her mind repeatedly were a few relics from ages past. One was the medieval Cloth of St Gereon, with its pattern of roundels enclosing the motif of a griffin and a bull in combat. It was, she recalled, a fragment of this precious woven fabric that she had been looking at in the South Kensington Museum of Art at the very moment when she and Kendrick met again after a long period of estrangement. But a different centuries-old textile tradition began to dominate her thinking as an inchoate embroidery design was starting to take shape. She saw how this tradition could furnish both an organising principle and a source for specific images. It was an insight that came as she stood again at the top of the main staircase, admiring those angular segments formed by intersections of the window's diagonal glazing bars. The pattern reminded her, not for the first time, of the diamond shapes in the border around that embroidered Icelandic bedspread she'd seen exhibited in London years before. She could visualise, too, the compelling array of figures stationed in rows inside the border, at once human and animal, combining bright and sombre colours, seeming simultaneously to invite and resist symbolic interpretation.

Her growing preoccupation with that old Icelandic style of adornment became more intense as the Gudrun story took a tighter hold. She found that lines and phrases from Morris's poem were dancing in her mind, and she would sometimes recite them under her breath as she scrubbed floors or washed dishes. *Interwoven miseries... Love slaying love, and ruinous victory... On unheard wings / The kestrel hangs above the mouse.* More and more the stark contours of that distant environment inhabited by the legendary Gudrun, Kiartan, Bodli and their kinsfolk seemed to Isabella like a dramatic analogue of the emotional world in which she herself, Kendrick, Barton and others had been living and moving. And now she saw how she could represent them all – lovers, friends, family – and the things they had meant to each other and done to each other. She could do it by deploying quasi-heraldic devices of the kind embroidered long ago by Icelandic artists.

Taking up needle and thread, she set to work on the task that she knew would be enormously demanding. Night by night, stitch by stitch, panel by panel, she transferred piecemeal to the coat a pattern that memory and imagination were combining to create. It needed to be done in the deepest recesses of the night, furtively, by dim candlelight. Her eyes ached from peering and squinting at the intricate details of her work. Although it required intense concentration, she could never let herself become completely absorbed in what she was doing, because as soon as she heard the approaching steps of an orderly doing the nocturnal rounds she had to be quick to snuff the candle and feign sleep before the inspection hatch on her door was pulled aside. Only when all was quiet could she light the candle again and resume her efforts. From time to time, as she worked, she would whisper phrases from Morris's poem, associating them in her mind with motifs that her needle was bringing into being.

Once or twice a faint whisper seemed to come to her in the darkness, questioning the point of it all. For whom was she executing this intricate work? *For nobody*, an inner voice answered defiantly. *For myself*.

The process was extremely slow, not only because some components of her design came together in a hesitant, gradual way and the craftwork techniques required painstaking effort but also because the supply of materials was intermittent. Although Tilly obligingly placed orders for whatever kinds and colours of thread and fabric Isabella asked for, these sometimes took a long while to arrive. Despite all the practical difficulties, it was deeply satisfying work. She gleaned a serene kind of delight from contemplating the emergence of what she had devised, a composition that brought together harmoniously a series of contrasts: the balancing of textures, the interplay of gloomy Norse elements with streaks of radiant austral colour, some as bright as parrot feathers. And for anyone skilled in discerning the relationships between certain images, there were hints of a half-hidden story for which she was both narrator and central character.

One alarming day, more than five years after her own committal to the Asylum, Isabella recognised that a new arrival was someone she had encountered before.

TWENTY-THREE

A FORTNIGHT AFTER THE FUNERAL, TILLY CARTER HEARD a knock and went to her front door. Runty Rowe stood there, rocking slightly from one short leg to the other. His thick streaky grey-and-white moustache overhung his mouth like a striped awning above a shop window.

'Inspector! Do come in. Well, this is a surprise. What brings you to Guildford?'

'Wanting to see you, Mrs Carter – sole purpose. I've come here to tell you what I've discovered about the fatal attack on your friend Miss Trent. Circumstances and culprit. I've already spoken to the Superintendent and Matron about my findings, and I'll soon complete a formal written report for Magistrate Fairbairn. But you're the person who knew her best, so it's only right to let you know personally what's now come to light.'

He sat stiff-backed in her parlour while she made a pot of tea, and then, curling stubby fingers around the delicate china cup handle and sipping noisily, he told her what facts he had been able to reconstruct and what remained a matter of conjecture.

❖

For nearly a week after the coronial inquest and the funeral, his investigation had made no progress. Though still convinced that Elsie Mack the absconding orderly was innocent of Isabella's murder, he had interrogated her for a second time, hoping for some detail that might lead him to the killer. Was there any particular patient, he wanted to know, who might have been aware of Mack's plan to slink away from the building, and perhaps able to observe her leaving the master key on the duty desk? Did Mack ever see signs of active hostility towards Trent on the part of patients or staff members? Did she remember any incident when Trent behaved in a way that could have made someone resentful or vengeful?

Mack's replies yielded nothing of interest at first. She did say that Trent reportedly had a reputation for fits of bad temper, which was why she was made to sleep in a solitary cell rather than in the general dormitory, though Mack herself never saw her express anger towards anyone. There had been a violent outburst from her a long time ago, years back, before Mack started work at the Asylum: people said that for some obscure reason Trent suddenly assaulted one of the harmless imbeciles, Alice Bradley. Mack thought this was odd because to her Trent seemed quiet and withdrawn.

'So I did briefly consider the possibility,' Inspector Rowe told Tilly Carter, 'that Alice Bradley, or perhaps some other inmate acting on her behalf, had killed Miss Trent in retaliation for that attack years before. But I dismissed the idea. Poor Alice seems incapable of holding a grudge, and the lapse of so much time since the assault makes it wholly improbable that anyone would want to avenge it now. However, in the course of further conversation, Elsie Mack happened to mention something else that gave me pause for thought.'

He went on to tell Tilly that Mack let slip an interesting fact about her fellow absconder, Thomas Ramsay: the night when she escaped with him was not the first time he had entered the women's part of the Asylum, and on the previous occasion he had menaced Isabella Trent. This occurred, Mack said, about a week before the pair of attendants decamped together. One afternoon when everybody was supposed to be out in the front garden getting fresh air and sunshine, she had unbolted a small side door and let him in through into the backyard. Although it was risky for him to enter the women's wing, he and Elsie needed to plan practical details of their intended departure, such as access to specific doors and exit routes. After quickly ascertaining that the arrangements they had in mind would be feasible after dark, Ramsay had taken the opportunity to pull her with him into a storeroom for what she blushingly told Inspector Rowe was 'a bit of a cuddle, hasty but lusty.' On emerging they were seen by Isabella Trent, who was loitering in the corridor after retreating indoors. Ramsay, snarling, had threatened Isabella with harm if she told anyone she had seen him in the women's wing.

Mack's account of this incident shifted Rowe's attention to Thomas Ramsay, who by now had been recaptured near Rockingham. In view of the possibility – most unlikely though it seemed – that Ramsay may have killed Trent to prevent her from telling anyone that she knew about his liaison with Mack, Rowe subjected him to intense questioning. But any notion of the former warder's responsibility for her death evaporated when Ramsay said sullenly he guessed 'that nebby meddler Trent' must have reported him after the escape – revealing he was unaware she had died.

Rowe's investigation took him along a different and more rewarding pathway, he said, after he pursued enquiries with a number of the inmates, one of whom mentioned that there was somebody in the Asylum who claimed to have come out to the colony on the same ship as Isabella Trent, and disliked her intensely. This person's name was Ruth Fitch.

Before proceeding to interview Fitch, he asked the Matron about her and then checked police records, which revealed that during her seven years in the colony she had become a troubled, volatile, unpredictable drunk. Frequent spasms of spite had often brought her to the attention of the law. Matron Higgs told him that Fitch, having repeatedly and viciously assaulted an elderly male neighbor after causing needless conflict with him, was admitted to the Asylum against her will. From the moment of her committal, Fitch had been belligerent. Other patients shrank from her and tried to keep their distance. Even Filthy Betty Philp soon learnt not to provoke her. So Ruth Fitch was being kept confined in a refractory cell.

Tilly Carter interrupted the Inspector's story at this point. 'It's surprising, isn't it, that the Matron said nothing about this violent troublemaker during the inquest, when she was asked about inmates who might have harmed Isabella?'

'I did raise that question with her,' replied Rowe. 'She said it hadn't occurred to her to mention Fitch because she wasn't aware of any contact between her and Miss Trent. Fitch has been locked away in her special padded cell for most of the time since her arrival, and Miss Trent, as you know, has generally been secluded too. Anyhow, I arranged to question Ruth Fitch...'

Rowe said that he saw at once why everyone gave Fitch a wide berth. Her whole manner was openly aggressive. She seemed intent on making trouble, regardless of consequences. Throughout his interview with her she had glared across the table, and at one stage threatened to strike him, bellowing, 'A clout with the flat of my hand, full force, won't leave a mark but I promise it will cause you pain.'

When Rowe casually dropped the name of Isabella Trent, Fitch made a derisive noise and described her sneeringly as 'that clever fool' whose cleverness had 'got her nowhere.' Asked bluntly whether she had killed Isabella, she laughed and spat, saying she would have liked to do so – but how could she, being imprisoned in her little cell at the time of the murder? 'They're all scared of me, see, so they put me in that special lockup out there in the yard, damn them. Like a mongrel in a kennel.'

Having once seen the notorious refractory cell, the Inspector could think of nobody more deserving to be its occupant, and said so to the Matron in conversation after his interview. 'I suppose,' he added, 'you keep Ruth Fitch in there permanently?'

'Not quite permanently, no. She's in that padded cell more often than not, but we don't like to think that anyone is incapable of reform. So we've let her back a couple of times into the general dormitory, though I must say the reprieve seldom lasts long.'

'Would your records show definitely where she was sleeping on the night of Miss Trent's death?'

'Perhaps. Let me consult the Occurrence Book.'

Matron Higgs fetched the large register and ran a finger over entries for the period in question. 'It appears that she was isolated in her usual cell... Ah, no – look – and I do remember this now! There's a note here, dated ten days ago: *Patient Ruth Fitch, having calmed down while confined for another week in R.C. –* that's the refractory cell – *is now being moved to dormitory on probation.* But then it's also recorded here that, after just a few nights in the dormitory, she started a fight and was put back into the solitary lockup.'

'So where was she on the night of the murder?'

'In the general dormitory, must have been.'

So Rowe had then questioned Fitch again, pointing out that the Occurrence Book showed clearly that she was not under lock and key when Trent was killed. He put it to her that she had left her dormitory bed to roam around, probably having heard the sounds of Mack's stealthy departure; that she had then found the keys lying on the unattended duty desk; that she used them to open Trent's cell door; and that she inflicted the mortal stab wound.

After staring at him coldly as he spoke, Fitch had given a scornful shrug and admitted with an air of nonchalance that he was right. Yes, it was her doing. Why? Because she'd hated Trent, she said, from the time when they were on the ship together. Hated her 'superior airs,' the way she kept aloof and acted as if domestic service was beneath her. Hated the fact that her voice had 'a ladylike tone.' Was sure there must be some secret, something she was hiding.

Then, on this fateful night, Fitch had purloined the keys and succeeded in surprising Isabella, unlocking her cell door to find her embroidering 'some ridiculous coat.' Fitch told Rowe that she felt enraged at discovering Trent's secret 'feminine' pastime. It made her wild to see this 'pretty ninny' toiling away by candle-light at 'one of those meek tasks that men expect women to submit to from our early years on, putting us to the needle as children.' It was disgusting that anyone would choose to under-take this kind of work. Trent had tried to defend stoutly what she was doing, Fitch said; a fierce argument had erupted between them, and Fitch, in a fury, seized the scissors and swung them into Trent's throat.

After Rowe finished his account of it all, he and Tilly sat in silence for a couple of minutes. She dabbed at her eyes with a handkerchief.

'A straightforward confession,' said Rowe. 'So the law will swiftly take its course.'

'Such a horrible way for Isabella's life to end!' Tilly said. 'After wasting away in her dark cell, year after year, to be cut short like that. So needlessly. So cruelly.' She lifted her hands in a half-shaped gesture of sorrow, and then let them drop into her lap.

'I'm thankful, Inspector,' she continued after a pause, 'that you've taken the trouble to come here and tell me what happened. There's a kind of peace in knowing you've solved the mystery of the poor woman's murder. But the mystery of her character remains, doesn't it? There's so much we'll never understand. What made her the person she was. How she developed that rare artistic talent of hers. What kind of life she led in England. Why she left it to come here.'

Rowe stroked his prodigious moustache. 'There were secrets, I'm sure. Fitch was right about that, and about glimpsing something that doesn't quite match a domestic service role. Knowing that Miss Trent grew up near to where I did, I wonder about her early years in that corner of Staffordshire. How they shaped her. The family and so forth.'

'She was such a strange mixture, wasn't she? Most of the time she seemed to have a kind of poise. Graceful, in a certain way. But occasionally there'd be a sudden outburst. You know about the incident when Isabella became very upset at a dance, and struck one of the other patients?' He nodded as she went on musing, 'What could have caused that, I wonder? And there was one time, while she was living in Guildford, when I was chattering away to her and said something about men, and she reacted quite sharply. I was taken aback. Some problem from the past, I suppose, gnawing at her.'

'Just one of the many things we'll never know about her background,' said Rowe. 'And now she's been flung into another unknown. The darkness that awaits us all.' He looked pensively into the fireplace, as if seeking answers there.

When Tilly spoke, her voice was tentative. 'It's like a parable of anyone's life, don't you think? Such a brief passage through the world. Such an untimely exit. We hardly have time to get to know ourselves, let alone anyone else.'

'Yes, yes. That's the truth of it. We're left with little more than a sense of... What? Baffled curiosity?'

'But although Isabella's life was so brief and sad, I don't see it as futile. That beautiful pattern she worked on with so much care: for reasons beyond our grasp, she's created something quite remarkable there. Something lasting. I was looking at it again just yesterday. Perhaps you'd like to see it before you go?'

She went to fetch the embroidered coat, and spread it reverently across the table. They stood before it in silence for a while, heads bowed as they gazed at the enigmatic images.

'It's ironical,' said Rowe, 'that what made Fitch so savagely angry, by her own admission, was the bee in her bonnet about needlework. She had a notion that it expresses womanly submission. She said your friend was passionate in arguing against that view. We can't know what words they exchanged, but my surmise is that Miss Trent would have defended what she was doing as a sort of...' He fingered his moustache again. 'As a creative use of a woman's private space.'

Tilly Carter cocked her head to one side like a foraging magpie. 'A woman's private space? What do you mean, Inspector?'

The effort of searching for the right words wrinkled his brow.

'While I don't pretend to grasp fully what this elaborate piece of embroidery may mean, I can recognise that it's artistry of a high order. No doubt men often like to decree and control what women should and shouldn't do, but when I look at this coat I see the work of someone who has tried to devise an alternative world where she isn't subject to the designs of any man.'

Tilly nodded slowly. *I shouldn't find it surprising, she thought, that a detective can be a philosopher.* They bent their heads over the coat again.

'So many puzzling details,' she said. Pointing to one of the central figures, she added, 'I've been wondering whether the strange shape beside this naked woman could be a watermill with a giant wheel. Yes? But if so, what might that mean?'

Ffiney Mede
1874

TWENTY-FOUR

As Midsummer's Day was approaching, young Lucy Malpass badgered her father about his promise to take her on a picnic excursion if the weather was fine.

'But *where* shall we go?'

He shrugged those big shoulders of his and took the clay pipe from his mouth. 'Oh, you can decide that, my dear. A twelve-year-old is surely entitled to make some choices. Just select any spot that our horse can take us to, and bring us back from, within a day.'

'But I don't know how far it is to anywhere. Tell me some good places for picnicking.'

Putting the newspaper aside, Henry Malpass looked up from his armchair.

'Well, let's see. We could go north of here, up to The Roaches. Part of the way on horseback, of course. After that there'd be some strenuous climbing. I think you'd enjoy a walk along the rocky ridge, and then there's a wonderful deep mossy cleft to explore, Lud's Church. We'd find a quiet cool nook in there for our picnic.'

'Aunt Barbara told me about Lud's Church. She says it's not a real church, it's a green ghost's haunt. I wouldn't like to meet a ghost.'

Henry Malpass chuckled. 'I don't know about ghosts, but Lud's Church can seem a gloomy place, that's true. And getting there would probably be tiring, even for a strong girl like you. You may prefer to go a few miles south, then. I know of a peaceful meadow, Ffiney Mede, right near the Cheddleton mills, between river and canal.'

'Mills? You mean there's more than one mill down there?'

'Both a flint mill – well, in fact it's a pair, on opposite banks of the river – and also an old silk mill close by. None of them in use these days.'

She clapped her hands. 'For a picnic, I like the idea of a meadow best. With old mills to look at.'

So it was decided.

The day before their planned outing, she studied the clouds anxiously. 'You said we can have our picnic "if the weather's fine" – but must it be really *very* fine?'

'Oh, just fine enough for us to enjoy ourselves. We don't want to get cold, do we?'

The dawn sky was cloudless, heralding one of the sunniest and most placid days of summer. Lucy packed a pork pie, a jar of stewed apple, a yeasty loaf of freshly baked bread and large chunks of Leek's best crumbly cheese. Henry Malpass added a few bottles of his favourite ale, brewed in Burton-on-Trent. 'Look at the gorgeous colour of it!' he exclaimed as he wrapped the bottles in cloth and put them into a saddlebag with the food. 'The county's very best barley wine.'

He saddled and bridled the bay gelding. 'Sturdy enough to carry us both, and more docile than my stallion.' Lucy perched in front, her father sitting close behind with his arms tightly around her as his large hands held the reins. She felt secure, safe, happy.

'How far is it?'

'A little more than three miles. We'll take it slowly.'

She leant back so that her head nestled against his chest and she could smell the pungent tobacco odour on his jacket. The steady rhythm of hooves and the warmth of the mid-morning sun on her cheek began to make her pleasantly drowsy. To keep herself awake, she prevailed upon her father to tell her more about their destination. Her insistent questions and his patient answers whiled away the travelling time. Why, she wanted to know, was it called Ffiney Mede? Oh, that's because the mede – the meadow – used to belong for many years to the Ffiney family, former owners of the flint mill. Why was the mill no longer in use? Because times were now so hard in the Potteries, reducing demand for flint. But what did the Potteries have to do with flint? Well, flint was crushed to a powder and mixed with clay to produce a cream-coloured earthenware, much sought-after. The mill, he told her, had probably been there for centuries, originally as a corn mill he'd wager, using the River Churnet as a ready source of water power – and then, with industry expanding in the Potteries, some clever fellow decided to adapt this mill because flint could be transported to and from the site on either the turnpike road or the Caldon Canal.

'You know so much! How did you find out all these things?'

'By putting endless questions to my elders, just as you're doing. The best way to learn. I'm glad you're full of curiosity, young lady. Keep up the questioning.'

So she asked him, too, about the silk mill at Cheddleton, and why it had stopped operating. The silk industry went into decline a few years back, he explained, and there were simply too many silk factories in the region, so competition drove some of them out of business. Yes, it was different now: Leek had a good number that were doing fairly well, such as his own. No, he didn't feel sad about the fact that the Cheddleton flint mill and silk mill were standing silent. They'd come to life again one day, he had no doubt. It wouldn't take much to get them back into working order. The site was so well suited to small industrial activity.

'People say, you know,' he added, 'that this place has been used for one kind of milling or another since Adam was a lad.'

'You mean the same Adam who's in the Bible? When was he a lad?'

'Long, long ago.'

'And when he was a lad, was Eve a lass?'

'Suppose so. I'm not the best person to ask, Lucy.'

'But you know how the Bible says that God made Eve out of Adam's rib…'

'Mmm?'

'Well, did he make her into a baby, or a grown-up person, or just a girl, like me?'

Laughing, her father shook his head. 'Don't know, my dear. You'd have to ask the vicar. He won't know either, but he'll surely invent some plausible answer.'

The sun was climbing high when they came over the small bridge near Cheddleton and arrived at the clump of old buildings. Beyond them she could see a meadow sloping towards the Churnet on one side with the canal on the other. Lifting Lucy down, Henry tethered the horse and ambled around the place with his daughter's hand in his, peering through windows and into cavities. To her delight, the flint mill was really two in one, just as he'd said: linked mills facing one another a few yards apart across the shared sluice, each with its own huge wheel to drive the machinery and provide water to mix with the milled particles. Beside the southbank mill were kilns for the preparatory process of calcining the flint to make it easier to crush and grind. Other structures stood nearby: an abandoned brewery, ramshackle stables, and the imposing former silk factory with its ground floor of solid stone and two further storeys of brick surmounted by a tapering chimney stack. 'Still equipped with spindles and looms, I'd wager,' said Henry Malpass after a cursory inspection from the outside. 'And when they finally closed its doors, perhaps even the steam engine that used to power it all may have been left in there too.'

Lucy lingered for a couple of minutes as she peered through a dusty window at a spider, intent on its dainty task. Painstakingly it was weaving a filamentary pattern across an upper corner of the glass. The cobweb tracery looked as delicate as the finest interlacing of silken threads.

They carried their food and drink to the meadow. Her father spread an old rug on a patch of riverside grass and cut slices of pie. She sat for a while in serene silence, chewing slowly as she listened to the faint sound of rippling water and watched the light dappling the walls of the mills. Small wings flickered through the air around them. Lucy asked, 'Were there chaffinches and butterflies in the Garden of Eden?'

'I can't tell you that,' said Henry Malpass, opening a second bottle of barley wine and wiping his lips with the back of his hand, 'but I will say this: any creatures in Eden must needs take care, for there'll always be a serpent lurking somewhere.'

She didn't believe that. A place as beautiful as this one was a carefree paradise. Wherever she looked, the scene was a panoply of colour: the scatterings of bright flowers across the grass, the speckle-feathered creatures in the air, the sun-soaked buildings with their pink brick and mottled stonework, the powder-blue sky reflected in the river. She would always remember this little world of pigmentary splendour.

The early afternoon heat was becoming oppressive. By now their feet were bare and Henry had also removed his jacket and rolled up his shirtsleeves. Lucy's bonnet shielded her face but made her scalp sweat. There was no shade except beside the buildings, where the dusty ground looked uncomfortable.

'Have a quick cooling swim, shall we?' he suggested. They walked over to the bank of the Churnet. She asked whether it was safe in the water and he reassured her. 'It's shallow on this side. You can paddle if you like. We'll be careful.'

They undressed, piled their clothes on the bank, and waded in. As she lowered herself into the clear water its coldness made her gasp, but it was bracing and she laughed at the sensation of the currents fondling her skin. Playfully he splashed water towards her. He had a surprising amount of hair on certain parts of his body. She looked away.

When they got out again they shook off as much water as possible and waited for the sun to dry their bodies. A slight breeze had come up. They shivered in their nakedness, but didn't want to dress while they were so wet.

'We need to do something to warm ourselves,' said her father. Still naked, he got down on hands and knees and told Lucy to climb onto his back, like riding a stallion. Or a stag. 'Imagine me with antlers.'

As she sat astride him, giggling, and he went crawling on all fours across the grass, he told her about the legendary Horn Dance held annually at Abbots Bromley, many a mile away in the southern part of the county. A friend of his, having seen it performed, had recounted what took place. The dancers, a group of a dozen men, wore masks and reindeer antlers as they wended their way through and around the village. Nobody knew what it signified but the tradition supposedly went back many centuries. Local people believed the Horn Dance had been brought to their part of England by Norse invaders.

'My knees are getting sore,' Henry said. She dismounted and he stood up.

'You make me think of the story of Lady Godiva,' he said. 'You know it, don't you?' She nodded. Then, gently, he clasped her. 'Stand on my feet.' She did, and he began a slow dance, swaying with her, the barley wine strong on his breath. Her feet were perched on his feet. Her cheek was against his chest and she heard the thump of his heart. She felt something odd and glanced down. A distinctive part of him had changed its shape and was brushing her front. She thought apprehensively of the bull she had once seen rampant in a cow-field.

She could not have said how long their strange dancing went on through that hot afternoon, but in the shadowland of her memory the sensations it induced would always linger. In a heavy silence they pulled their clothes on and gathered up the picnic remnants. As their horse took them homeward she kept her hands clenched, holding tightly not only to its mane but also to the confusions of the day, the things that had made her laugh and the things that brought twinges of uneasy excitement. She was unsure whether she was keeping them all in her grip, or they were clutching her. Every distinctive detail of light and shade, of colour and pattern, of water and meadow, of food and drink, of feathers and flowers, of rectangular buildings and great round wheels, of splashing and dancing, of fibrous clothes and bare flesh: in all its enchanting, disturbing particulars, that day on Ffiney Mede was going to stay with her until the very end of her life.

AFTERWORD

*T*HE *MADWOMAN'S COAT* IS A WORK OF FICTION. MOST OF those who inhabit the foregoing pages, including the main character, are entirely invented. A few, though reshaped by my imagination, have real-life historical counterparts, as their recognisable names plainly indicate – the Morris family and their associates are obvious examples – and many aspects of my novel reflect actual historical situations, practices, episodes and institutions. To create a factual framework for this fictitious story, I made use of various resources, both archival and published. Some of the groundwork was done during my tenure of a J.S. Battye Memorial Fellowship awarded by the State Library of Western Australia, which gave me ready access to all sorts of stimulating material (from maps and photographs to pamphlets, typescripts and newspaper reports) that I might not have discovered otherwise. For the Battye Library's generous support and professional expertise my warm thanks go to Margaret Allen, Susanna Iuliano, Kate Gregory and Theresa Archer. In connection with that fellowship I was also fortunate to receive practical help from Gerard Foley in delving into valuable manuscript and microfilm holdings in the State Records Office, such as Occurrence Books and other registers from the Fremantle Lunatic Asylum. Sheridan Coleman of the Fremantle Arts Centre (the former Asylum site) provided me with historical information about the building and showed me some of the areas not open to the general public; I thank her for this kindness.

In addition, I gratefully acknowledge here the use I have made of published research by a large number of scholars. The following books and journal articles were, for my purposes, particularly informative on the subject of asylums for the mentally ill: Charlotte MacKenzie, *Psychiatry for the Rich: A history of Ticehurst Private Asylum, 1792-1917*; Alannah Tomkins, *Medical Misadventure in an Age of Professionalisation: 1780-1890*; Jane Hall, *May They Rest in Peace: The history and ghosts of the Fremantle Lunatic Asylum*; Bronwyn Harman, 'Women and Insanity: The Fremantle Asylum in Western Australia, 1858-1908,' in Penelope Hetherington and Philippa Maddern (eds), *Sexuality and Gender in History*; Jennifer Carter, *Eyes to the Future: Sketches of Australia and her Neighbours in the 1870s* (chapter on 'Our Lunatic Asylums'); and essays by Roger Virtue, Norman Megahey and Margaret McPherson in *Studies in Western Australian History* (nos. 1, 14 and 24 respectively).

On various aspects of the Morris circle, the Arts and Crafts movement, the Royal School of Art Needlework and related topics, I consulted many sources but am especially grateful for insights gleaned from contemporary publications such as May Morris's *Decorative Needlework* (1893) and Lady Marian Alford's *Needlework as Art* (1886), as well as a number of later works, most notably A.S. Byatt, *Peacock and Vine*; Anthea Callen, *Angel in the Studio: Women in the Arts and Crafts Movement*;

Lara Kriegel, *Grand Designs: Labor, Empire and the Museum in Victorian Culture*; Jan Marsh, *Jane and May Morris: A biographical story*; Joseph Baylen, 'George Bernard Shaw and the Socialist League,' *International Review of Social History* 7.3; Linda Parry (ed.), *William Morris: Art and Kelmscott*; David Saxby, *William Morris at Merton*; Paul Thompson, *The Work of William Morris*; the multi-volume *Collected Works of William Morris*, edited by May Morris; the multi-volume *Collected Letters of William Morris* edited by Norman Kelvin; and that great treasure trove, Fiona MacCarthy's biography *William Morris*.

For further information about particular traditions and practices of embroidery, I wish to thank Cathryn Walton, *Hidden Lives: Leek's extraordinary embroiderers* (and Cathryn also kindly corresponded with me in response to specific research questions of mine); Carola Hicks, *The Bayeux Tapestry: The life story of a masterpiece*; Elsa E. Guthjónsson, *Traditional Icelandic Embroidery*; and Maureen Daly Goggin and Beth Fowkes Tobin (eds), *Women and the Material Culture of Needlework and Textiles, 1750-1950*.

For details about railway topics relevant to my story I acknowledge the work of Jack Simmons and Gordon Biddle (eds), *The Oxford Companion to British Railway History*; Jeffrey Richards and John M. Mackenzie, *The Railway Station: A social history*; Gordon Biddle and O.S. Nock, *The Railway Heritage of Britain: 150 Years of railway architecture and engineering*; and David Welsh, *Underground Writing: The London Tube from George Gissing to Virginia Woolf*.

I found rich historical information about certain places where parts of my story are set, such as Leek, South Kensington and New Swindon, in British History Online (http://www.british-history.ac.uk), while for specialised aspects of particular heritage sites and traditional practices I was glad to rely on Harry Jones, *East and West London*, Robert Copeland, *A Short History of Pottery Raw Materials and the Cheddleton Flint Mill*, and Robert Faulkner, *Icelandic Men and Me*.

On the Third Anglo-Burmese war there are fine historical accounts in print, most notably A.T.Q. Stewart, *The Pagoda War*; but I also found the photographs of Willoughby Wallace Hooper remarkably illuminating, and accessible through an excellent British Library site – http://www.bl.uk/onlinegallery. About the British Army in that period I learned a good deal from Myna Trustram, *Women of the Regiment: Marriage and the Victorian Army*; Heather Streets, *Martial Races: The military, race and British imperial culture*; and Gwyn Harries-Jenkins, *The Army in Victorian Society*.

For fascinating details about nineteenth-century migration by women, I am indebted to Jan Gothard, *Blue China: Single female migration to colonial Australia*, and a pair of articles by Tricia Fairweather and Leonie Hayes, 'Bride Ships in all but Name: Miss Monk and the servant girls,' *Western Ancestor* 12.6 and 12.7.

To the National Museum of Iceland, Reykjavik (particularly Kristin Halla Baldvinsdóttir) and the Pennsylvania Academy for the Fine Arts, Philadelphia (particularly Danielle McAdams) I express my gratitude for kind permission to use the images reproduced on the cover. Details of the respective works are: Riddarateppid (Coverlet of Knights), 17th century, unknown provenance, embroidered with multi-coloured woollen yarn on a woollen ground in an extended tabby weave; and Susan Macdowell Eakins, 'Woman Sewing' (c. 1880), oil on canvas, Charles Bregler's Thomas Eakins Collection, purchased with the support of the Pew Memorial Trust and the Henry C. Gibson Fund.

Afterword

And above all, for various kinds of personal encouragement, my heartfelt thanks go to Brian Edwards, Robyn Gardner, Paul Genoni, Nicholas Hasluck, Dorte Heurlin, Lorraine Jacobs, Ali Jaquet, Yvonne Laing, Iris Lavell, Gale MacLachlan, Linda Martin, Edith Moore, Clive Newman, Marian Novick, Ken Spillman, Michael Stanford, Anthony Styan, Tangea Tansley, Andrew Taylor, Brenda Walker and Bob White.